Praise for
Unstuck

"For years now, Barbara Dee has written one exceptional novel after another. *Unstuck* may be her best yet. Lyla's story is at once unique and universal, and readers will finish the book feeling inspired and empowered to take control of, and share, their stories."
—Jarrett Lerner, author of *A Work in Progress*

"A wonderful, heartfelt and honest story about trying to write a novel and survive middle school, *Unstuck* is this generation's *Dear Mr. Henshaw*."
—Kirby Larson, author of Newbery Honor Book *Hattie Big Sky*

"Lyla is a character to root for! Her battle with writer's block and her journey to overcome it are both relatable and inspiring. With family and friendship relationships weaved in, *Unstuck* is an entertaining and heartfelt read."
—Janae Marks, *New York Times* bestselling author of *On Air With Zoe Washington*

"A portrait of a writer as a seventh grader! Humorous, heart-warming, and oh-so-real, *Unstuck* shows us how surviving middle school is a lot like the craft of writing. We must accept that it isn't easy, it helps to have friends, and, above all, we have to stay true to ourselves. Word lovers and budding novelists will love this book—but so will anyone who is, will soon be, or once was an adolescent."
—Jennifer Ziegler, author of *Worser*

"*Unstuck* joyfully celebrates the complex writing process and empowers young readers with the knowledge that creativity is a personal journey and sometimes strength is found in unexpected places."
—Veera Hiranandani, author of *How to Find What You're Not Looking For* and *The Night Diary*, a Newbery Honor Book

"With her trademark humor and warmth, Barbara Dee has crafted an empowering story about creativity, self-esteem, and the pressures that come along with pursuing a passion. Dee incorporates writing strategies that will inspire budding authors and delight English teachers, and Lyla's deeply relatable journey will resonate with anyone who's ever felt stuck—whether they're battling writer's block, navigating changing friendships, or yearning to emerge from a sibling's shadow."
—Laurie Morrison, author of *Up for Air* and *Coming Up Short*

"With perfect storytelling, Barbara Dee's latest novel is an honest look at finding the courage to push forward in the complexities of friendship, family, creativity, and truth— even when it seems impossible."
—Chris Barron, author of *All of Me* and *The Magical Imperfect*

"In *Unstuck*, Barbara Dee writes with an uncondescending and inspiring honesty that captures the highs, lows, and in-betweens of the creative process. This book is a gift to young readers and a valentine to young writers everywhere."
—Chris Tebbetts, co-author of the Middle School series with James Patterson and author of *Me Myself & Him*

Praise for
Haven Jacobs Saves the Planet

"Once again, Barbara Dee has created vivid, real, likable middle school characters who tackle big problems. Full of humor, science, and activism, *Haven Jacobs Saves the Planet* addresses the eco-anxiety that many young people feel. Readers will cheer for Haven and her friends as they navigate complicated friendships and act to help save their town's river . . . and, just maybe, the planet."
—Rajani LaRocca, author of Newbery Honor Book
Red, White, and Whole

"Relatable, achingly imperfect, and inspiringly hopeful, Barbara Dee's characters jump off the page. Readers will cheer for Haven as she discovers that—in spite of our fears—we all have the ability to do small things greatly."
—Jodi Lynn Anderson, bestselling author
of *My Diary from the Edge of the World* and
the Thirteen Witches trilogy

"An empathetic exploration of youth eco-anxiety that provides comfort, hope, and ways to cope in an uncertain world. Barbara Dee's deeply developed and beautifully flawed characters navigate the ups and downs of friendships and family relationships as they face a local environmental crisis head-on in this crucial, timely, and engaging novel."
—Lisa McMann, *New York Times* bestselling author
of the Unwanteds series

"I loved this book! *Haven Jacobs* is full of heart, healing, and hope. This story will leave readers inspired, energized, and ready to change the world."
—Carrie Firestone, author of *Dress Coded*
and *The First Rule of Climate Club*

"Dynamic, engaging, and full of heart, *Haven Jacobs Saves the Planet* is the voice of a generation of kids who care deeply about the environment and want to put hope into action."
—**Chris Baron, author of *All of Me* and *The Magical Imperfect***

"As readers keep turning the pages of this accessible and immediately engaging narrative, they will discover in Haven Jacobs a relatable, believable protagonist with an indefatigable spirit."
—**Padma Venkatraman, author of *Born Behind Bars* and *The Bridge Home***

"A powerful and pitch-perfect story that will inspire readers to take action and fight for change."
—**Alyson Gerber, author of *Taking Up Space* and *Focused***

A 2021 SLJ Best Book

Praise for
Violets Are Blue

"*Violets Are Blue* will break your heart and then piece it back together with infinite care. Barbara Dee expertly captures the struggle to be known and loved within a narrative that presents the complicated reality of addiction. Both Wren and her mother will stay with you long after this story is done."
—Jamie Sumner, author of *Roll with It* and *Tune It Out*

"Barbara Dee tunes into issues that impact middle schoolers and writes about them with compassion, insight, and just plain excellent storytelling. I loved this absorbing, accessible novel, which explores the heartbreaking effects of opioid addiction while also celebrating the joys of discovering a passion and finding people who understand you."
—Laurie Morrison, author of *Up for Air* and *Saint Ivy*

"Barbara Dee has done it again! *Violets Are Blue* is an emotionally rich story that masterfully weaves life's messy feelings while gently and thoughtfully tackling the difficult subject of opioid addiction. Beautiful. Complicated. And full of heart. A must read!"
—Elly Swartz, author of *Smart Cookie* and *Dear Student*

"Told realistically and with compassion, *Violets Are Blue* provides a fascinating look into the world of special effects makeup, budding friendships, family, and the secrets we keep."
—Melanie Sumrow, author of *The Inside Battle* and *The Prophet Calls*

A 2021 SLJ Best Book
A Project LIT Book Club selection
A Junior Library Guild Selection
A Cybils Awards Finalist
One of A Mighty Girl's 2021 Books of the Year

Praise for
My Life in the Fish Tank

"I loved *My Life in the Fish Tank*. Once again, Barbara Dee writes about important topics with intelligence, nuance, and grace. She earned all the accolades for *Maybe He Just Likes You* and will earn them for *My Life in the Fish Tank* too."

—Kimberly Brubaker Bradley, author of Newbery Honor Books *Fighting Words* and *The War That Saved My Life*

"I felt every beat of Zinny Manning's heart in this authentic and affecting story. Barbara Dee consistently has her finger on the pulse of her middle-grade audience. Outstanding!"

—Leslie Connor, author of *A Home for Goddesses and Dogs* and National Book Award finalist *The Truth as Told by Mason Buttle*

"*My Life in the Fish Tank* is a powerful portrayal of a twelve-year-old dealing with her sibling's newly discovered mental illness. Author Barbara Dee deftly weaves in themes of friendship, family, and secrets, while also reminding us all to accept what we can't control. I truly loved every moment of this emotional and gripping novel, with its notes of hope that linger long after the last page."

—Lindsay Currie, author of *The Peculiar Incident on Shady Street* and *Scritch Scratch*

"*My Life in the Fish Tank* rings true for its humor, insight, and honesty. Zinny is an appealing narrator, and her friendships with supporting characters are beautifully drawn."

—Laura Shovan, author of *Takedown* and *A Place at the Table*

"Barbara Dee offers a deeply compassionate look at life for twelve-year-old Zinny, whose older brother faces mental health challenges. This touching novel will go a long way in providing understanding and empathy for young readers. Highly recommended."
—Donna Gephart, award-winning author of *Lily and Dunkin* and *Abby, Tried and True*

A Bank Street Best Book of the Year
A Junior Library Guild Selection
One of A Mighty Girl's 2020 Books of the Year

Praise for
Maybe He Just Likes You

"Mila is a finely drawn, sympathetic character dealing with a problem all too common in middle school. Readers will be cheering when she takes control! An important topic addressed in an age-appropriate way."
—**Kimberly Brubaker Bradley, author of Newbery Honor Books**
Fighting Words **and** *The War That Saved My Life*

"In *Maybe He Just Likes You*, Barbara Dee sensitively breaks down the nuances of a situation all too common in our culture—a girl not only being harassed, but not being listened to as she tries to ask for help. This well-crafted story validates Mila's anger, confusion, and fear, but also illuminates a pathway towards speaking up and speaking out. A vital read for both girls and boys."
—**Veera Hiranandani, author of Newbery Honor Book** *The Night Diary*

"Mila's journey will resonate with many readers, exploring a formative and common experience of early adolescence that has too often been ignored. Important and empowering."
—**Ashley Herring Blake, author of Stonewall Children's & Young Adult Honor Book** *Ivy Aberdeen's Letter to the World*

"*Maybe He Just Likes You* is an important, timeless story with funny, believable characters. Mila's situation is one that many readers will connect with. This book is sure to spark many productive conversations."
—**Dusti Bowling, author of** *Insignificant Events in the Life of a Cactus*

"In this masterful, relatable, and wholly unique story, Dee shows how one girl named Mila finds empowerment, strength, and courage within. I loved this book."
—**Elly Swartz, author of** *Smart Cookie* **and** *Dear Student*

"*Maybe He Just Likes You* is the perfect way to jump-start dialogue between boy and girl readers about respect and boundaries. This book is so good. So needed! I loved it!"
—**Paula Chase, author of *So Done* and *Keeping It Real***

A Washington Post Best Children's Book
An ALA Notable Children's Book
A Project LIT Book Club selection
A Bank Street Best Book of the Year
An ALA Rise: A Feminist Book Project selection

ALSO BY BARBARA DEE

Haven Jacobs Saves the Planet

Violets Are Blue

My Life in the Fish Tank

Maybe He Just Likes You

Everything I Know About You

Halfway Normal

Star-Crossed

Truth or Dare

The (Almost) Perfect Guide to Imperfect Boys

Trauma Queen

This Is Me From Now On

Solving Zoe

Just Another Day in My Insanely Real Life

UNSTUCK

BARBARA DEE

ALADDIN
NEW YORK LONDON TORONTO SYDNEY NEW DELHI

ALADDIN

An imprint of Simon & Schuster Children's Publishing Division
1230 Avenue of the Americas, New York, New York 10020
First Aladdin hardcover edition February 2024
Text copyright © 2024 by Barbara Dee
Jacket illustration copyright © 2024 by Erika Pajarillo
All rights reserved, including the right of reproduction in whole or in part in any form.
ALADDIN and related logo are registered trademarks of Simon & Schuster, LLC
Simon & Schuster: Celebrating 100 Years of Publishing in 2024
For information about special discounts for bulk purchases, please contact Simon & Schuster Special Sales at 1-866-506-1949 or business@simonandschuster.com.
The Simon & Schuster Speakers Bureau can bring authors to your live event.
For more information or to book an event contact the Simon & Schuster Speakers Bureau at 1-866-248-3049 or visit our website at www.simonspeakers.com.
Designed by Heather Palisi and Ginny Chu
The text of this book was set in Odile.
Manufactured in the United States of America 0124 BVG
2 4 6 8 10 9 7 5 3 1
CIP data for this book is available from the Library of Congress.
ISBN 9781534489868 (hc)
ISBN 9781534489882 (ebook)

To my family, always there for me when I get stuck

THE BLANK PAGE

Okay, here we go.

What I've been waiting for, the chance to share my story. Not just the random bits I've been writing in my head, or scribbling on notepads, but the whole thing, from the absolute beginning.

I mean, I *guess* from the absolute beginning.

Because . . . what exactly *is* the absolute beginning? The day Aster is born? Or runs away from home? Or first spies the one-toed Beast that's tracking her every move? But so much happens *before* all that, and it's stuff I should probably explain in the first chapter. Seriously, if you don't know about the Defectors, or Oleander the Witch, or how Aster's big sister is basically kidnapped, nothing in the plot will make any sense.

And this story gets incredibly complicated, although in a good way. Really, there's so much action, it could be a whole series! I wonder if Ms. Bowman would let me keep writing. I bet she would, once she sees how much there is to tell, because she's the kind of teacher who lets you actually *create*. Unlike Mr. Delgado last year, who made us write five-paragraph essays on topics like Why Kids Need Limits on Screen Time. I mean literally—*five paragraphs*, not four or six. Once I actually wrote seven paragraphs and he made me smoosh them together so that I had exactly five. It's amazing I survived sixth grade without my brain leaking out my ears.

And now Ms. Bowman is smiling in my direction. Making eye contact and nodding like, *Go ahead, Lyla. Why don't you start writing?*

I smile back at her like, *No problem! Here I go! Writing my story!*

Seriously, Ms. Bowman is the coolest teacher in the entire school, even if she thought my sister, Dahlia, was a genius. But I don't hold it against her, because teachers *always* think Dahlia is a genius. It's what my parents think too. And of course Dahlia agrees with all of them.

Anyway.

I click the top of my favorite gel pen: blue ink, extra-fine tip, not too clunky in my hand. When Ms. Bowman told us about daily writing, some kids said they could write only on their laptops. Ms. Bowman said she'd like us to begin our stories in spiral notebooks, although later on we can switch to tablets or computers, if we want. But I don't think I will, at least not until I have a first draft. I like to feel a pen in my hand, and see my handwriting on the paper. It just seems, I don't know, more personal somehow.

And the thought that soon, in maybe just a few weeks, this empty notebook will be *completely filled*—every page, every line—makes me feel like dancing. Of course I stay in my seat, but it's hard to stop smiling. Not that you need to suffer to write a story! I mean, that's such a cliché, right? Why can't writing just make you happy?

In front of me, Stella Ramirez is using a pencil, and so is Noah Hennessey on my right. Stella's pencil is one of those fancy mechanical ones, but Noah's is a nub, barely big enough to grip. I watch them both hunch over their desks, doing two different kinds of hunching. Stella sits like she's taking a test, and doesn't want anyone copying her answers. Noah is hunched like he's already given up, even though we're just getting started.

Poor Noah—he looks so miserable. In math class he knows all the answers, so I bet he likes numbers better than words. I'm the total opposite: if I could do nothing all day long except reading and writing, I'd be the happiest human on the planet!

CHAPTER ONE

This story will have lots of chapters, so they'll definitely need numbers. I wonder how many there'll be by the last page of this notebook, because it's going to be *extremely long*. Way longer than five paragraphs—so DO NOT READ THIS, Mr. Delgado! Nothing to see here, hahaha!

Although later on I *might* give the chapters titles instead of numbers. Possibly. I haven't decided—but that's okay, because there's plenty of time to think about things like that. We're going to be working on this writing project for the next few weeks, Ms. Bowman says. Every day, for at least a few minutes! Woohoo!

Seriously, Ms. Bowman is like the Best Teacher Ever. I can barely wait to see her reaction when she reads this! When I'm ready to show it to her, I mean.

Oh no. Wait, stop!

Why is my hand all blue?

Is that *ink*?

Oh crap, my pen is leaking!

Gross! Just as I was getting started!

I'd better go wash up in the bathroom.

Even if the period is basically over now, and I won't have time to do any writing.

INK POISONING

Right after ELA is lunch. Like usual, I sit with Journey Lombardi-Sullivan. One day at the start of seventh grade she just decided that we would sit together, and I was too surprised by this to argue. So now that's what we do every day.

Back in elementary school, I always ate lunch with my best friend, Rania Goswami. But the way our town works, starting in sixth grade half the kids from our elementary school go to Walt Whitman Middle School and the other half go to Emily Dickinson. And since Rania lives on the north side of town, she goes to Dickinson. I go to Whitman, along with no one I'm actually friends with.

Unless you count Journey, who's a nice person, but a little . . . weird. I mean, I think it's cool that her dream job is to work in the control room at NASA. I like hearing about all her pets—a corn snake, a ferret, a bearded dragon, some rabbits, a box turtle, and an axolotl. I don't mind that she always wears a chocolate-brown newsboy cap indoors (unless a teacher makes her take it off). I don't even mind the way she hums (softly, just loud enough that you can tell she's off-key). But sometimes having a normal conversation with her isn't easy.

For example, today. I'm telling her about my story— what I'm deciding about the characters—and she isn't saying anything, or asking questions. But she's eating her big, drippy taco like she forgot to have breakfast.

"And when Aster discovers what's happened to her big sister, she leaves home to rescue her," I explain.

Journey doesn't say anything. Some cheddar cheese escapes from her taco; she pokes it back in with her thumb. Is she even listening? It's hard to tell.

"So that's why she has to battle through the Quagmire," I add. "Which is haunted by the Defectors. And other creatures too, like a mysterious one-toed Beast."

BARBARA DEE

"Huh," Journey says finally. "Why can't Aster just fly over it?"

"Excuse me?"

"The Quagmire, I mean. Didn't you say she had wings?"

"No. Where'd you get *that*?"

"Oh, sorry. I thought that's what you said."

"Journey, Aster's a person, not a dragon. Or a bird—"

"Sorry, Lyla. I like comics, but I don't read a whole lot of fantasy." Journey tugs on the brim of her newsboy cap. She used to have hair down to her butt until one day in sixth grade, when she cut it off to donate to Locks of Love. Now what's left of her almost-blond hair practically disappears under her cap. Except for her bangs, which she didn't cut at all.

Sometimes I think about chopping off my hair for a good cause. But it's thick and shiny, the kind of brown that changes color in the sunlight. I've spent the past two years growing it past my shoulders—and with my pale, round cheeks, gray eyes, and blobby nose, it's the only thing about my looks I actually like.

"Can I ask you a personal question, Lyla?" Journey says as she wipes her mouth with a greasy napkin. "Why are your hands all purple?"

8

"They're not," I say. "My pen leaked blue ink, and I washed it off. Mostly."

"Well, don't put your fingers in your mouth or you'll get ink poisoning."

"Ink poisoning?"

"Yeah, if you swallow Sharpie it's toxic. But you have to eat large quantities to actually die. I read an article."

That's another thing about Journey: one of her hobbies is reading random stuff online and then telling you about it. Even when you kind of wish she wouldn't.

I nibble my tuna sandwich. "Well, don't worry, okay? Anyhow, the ink isn't from a Sharpie."

"The article said *any* ink could be toxic. In biggish amounts."

"Okay, thanks." I say this because I don't know what else to say.

Then I tell myself that I'll just call Rania tonight, because *she'll* want to hear my story. And actually *listen* when I describe the plot.

Maybe she'll even suggest a great way to begin.

PARACHUTE

At dinner, Mom passes the salad bowl to Dahlia, who immediately passes the bowl to me.

"Aren't you having any?" Mom asks my sister.

Dahlia shakes her head.

"Why not?" Dad asks.

"My stomach feels funny," Dahlia says.

Mom frowns. "What does that mean? How is it funny?"

"Just nervous or something. I don't know. But I definitely shouldn't have any salad."

Dad dumps half a bottle of ranch dressing on his lettuce. "What are you nervous about, baby?"

He calls her that even though she's seventeen and a senior in high school. And with her bouncy blond hair, big green eyes, and high cheekbones, she looks like a TikTok star, not a kid, and definitely not a baby.

"I don't know," Dahlia says again. She takes a bite of roll. "The whole college thing, I guess. All the applications."

I chew a naked slice of cucumber. I never use salad dressing; to me it's like drowning your vegetables in oily soup.

"You started working on the essay?" Mom asks my sister.

"Eh," Dahlia says. "Sort of."

"Because with those schools you're looking at, it's really so important! A great college essay can make a huge difference."

Dahlia tears off a chunk of roll. "Mom, I *know*."

"And even with your grades—"

"Megan, she said she knows," Dad says.

"Well, there's knowing and there's actually doing something about it," Mom replies.

Nobody talks for a minute. Underneath the table our scruffy dog, Spumoni, pokes my foot, like he's giving me a cue to talk.

So I do. "We started writing stories in ELA," I announce. "Ms. Bowman says we'll do a little every day. And it's creative, so it can be about anything."

Mom and Dad look at me like I've just parachuted down to the dinner table. Like they're trying to remember who I am and how I got there.

"Fun," Dad says with too much enthusiasm. "What's your story about, Ly?"

I crunch on a crouton. "Well, it's a fantasy novel, and it gets really complicated. Mostly it's about these two sisters, and they live in a world where kids get sorted out, and then assigned to these jobs for the rest of their lives. So like the older sister gets assigned Vanguard, and the younger sister gets Scribe. At first the younger sister is kind of jealous, because Vanguard is supposed to be the best, and Scribe just means writing things, lists and contracts and recipes and boring stuff like that. But then the younger sister finds out what Vanguard really is—basically a sacrifice during war—and she has to rescue the older one. Which means she has to cross the Quagmire and battle enemies. Who are all hunting her down for some reason she doesn't understand."

"Enemies?" Dad drinks some water.

"Yeah, a one-toed Beast that's kind of stalking her for some reason. And a bunch of witches. Also the Defectors, who used to be people who tried to rebel, until they got caught and were turned into these horrible Quagmire creatures. Who shriek."

"Wow. Sounds exciting."

"I haven't worked out all the details yet," I say. "But it can be as long as we want. Mine may even end up a whole series."

"A *series*?" Dahlia says.

"Yeah. Lots of fantasy novels are series. Percy Jackson, *The City of Ember*—"

"Lyla, I *know*. I just meant a series is a lot of writing."

"Not for me! I'm always writing anyway."

Dahlia's eyebrows shoot up. "You are? Since when?"

The question stings.

Because doesn't she know how much I love words? How I'm always reading—and thinking about—stories? And filling up notebooks with amazing ideas? I even got in trouble for it in ELA last June, when Mr. Delgado checked our writing notebooks, and instead of some boring exactly-five-paragraph essay about Why You Should Study a Foreign Language, I'd written a two-page tour of the Quagmire, with maps and pictures.

And I mean, Dahlia is *my sister*, so she should have noticed this about me! Because it's basically who I *am*.

So then I wonder: *Do Mom and Dad know this about me? Does anyone?*

Well, Rania does. And Journey, too, I guess, because I've told her. If she was even listening . . .

I shrug like: *Ho-hum, Dahlia, you can't insult me.* "Well, I first started thinking about this story last spring. Mostly I've just been planning little scenes in my head. And writing a whole novel will be totally different, but I've already started, so."

"I'm sure your story will be *excellent*, Lyla," Mom says. "I can't wait to read it."

She slices a tomato with a steak knife. I almost ask how she's sure it will be excellent if she hasn't even read it. But I stop myself.

The table goes quiet.

Dahlia chews her roll like she's thinking something. Then she flips her hair over one shoulder, looks at me through her long eyelashes, and sighs.

"Oh, Lyla," she says. "You're so lucky you're just in seventh grade."

FLOWERS

After Dahlia and I clear the table, I go upstairs to my room. I sit at my desk and open my math textbook so it looks like I'm doing homework. When I hear Mom close the door to the bathroom, I text Rania: HEY.

I wait twenty-three minutes, then text again. HEY, IT'S ME. You there???

Still no answer.

Probably she's eating supper, even though it's almost seven thirty. By now I've gotten used to the fact that Rania's family is on a different schedule from mine. Her parents usually get home from work pretty late, and sometimes they don't start supper until eight or eight thirty. So there's no point calling her, because Rania's parents don't allow phones at the table.

I know she'll text back as soon as she can, because she always does. But I wish she'd just answer already.

Bleh.

Well, maybe while I'm waiting I should start my math homework. Although just thinking about exponents gives me a brain-ache. And all I *really* want to work on is my story, even though we're only supposed to do it at school.

Ms. Bowman was very clear about that: "Listen up, cats and kittens," she told us. "This is an ongoing class project, not a homework assignment. So please leave your writing notebooks on my desk at the end of class, okay?"

"Are you going to read what we write?" Noah asked. He looked worried.

"Not unless you're ready to share it with me," Ms. Bowman said. "Although I *will* be checking your progress from time to time."

When she said this, I wanted to ask if we were *allowed* to work on it at home. I mean, if we *chose* to. Because then it wouldn't be homework, just voluntary. But I didn't want her to think I was challenging her, especially since she was letting us be creative, woohoo! So I left my spiral notebook on her desk, just like everybody else.

What I'm thinking now is that even if I'm not actually writing in my writing notebook, I can still do *something* useful, right? Like researching names for my characters. Because names are super important! Sometimes I stop reading books when the names feel all wrong for the characters. And in my story I've decided that the main character is called Aster, so it would be good if her older sister had a flower name too—maybe a more show-offy kind of flower than aster. But not Dahlia, obviously. Anything but Dahlia.

I open my laptop and type: *girl names flower.*

What comes up: *Fifty Adorable Flower Names for Your Baby Girl.* Aster's older sister is fourteen—not a baby, obviously—but maybe some of these names would work.

I scroll through the list, which includes *Country of Origin, Meaning, This Name in Popular Culture,* and *Celebrity Babies with This Name* (like anyone cares). Except it's all Rose, Iris, Daisy, Posy, Lily. Regular, normal names, not names for fantasy characters!

I type something else: *Weird Flower Names.*

This list is way shorter: *Bat Face Cuphea. Naked Man Orchid. Eyeball Plant—*

Okaayyy, a little *too* weird.

How about: *Unusual Flower Names.* Because "unusual" is not the same as "weird."

Common Toadflax, Swamp Lousewort, Thimbleweed, Cheeseweed, Corn-cockle, Pussytoes, Adder's Tongue, Sneeze-weed, Turtlehead, Mad Dog Skullcap, False Hellebore, Viper's Bugloss, Monkeyflower, Cow Vetch—

Haha, these are awesome! Although completely wrong for Aster's sister, obviously. Maybe for other characters, though—possibly low-level villains, like assistants to the witches. Or the king's minions:

Cheeseweed, fetch me my sword!

Turtlehead, what have you done! And where's Pussytoes with my cape?

You can't hide from me, Cow Vetch! Even here, in the Quag-mire!

Ooh, I'm so in love with these names! I'll copy them on a Post-it and add them to my writing notebook tomorrow. Maybe I'll start a list of cool names on the back page.

Yay! Progress!

Although I still need a name for Aster's sister. Right now I'm thinking she's the favorite daughter—beautiful, obedient, and boring. Has perfectly straight long blond hair she spends a lot of time brushing. Never argues, never fights back. A good student—although not as brilliant as

Aster, who annoys her tutor with too many questions. And refuses to follow directions. And doesn't care that she's kind of plain-looking and messy.

In a lot of ways, Aster and her sister are total opposites. But since they're sisters, they do need names that go together. Kind of.

I type: *Unique Flower Names.* Because "unique" is not the same as "weird." Or "unusual."

What comes up: *Acacia. Hyacinth. Tulip. Verbena. Clover. Myrtle—*

Okay, so now we're getting somewhere! Myrtle sounds like a wrinkly old lady who stinks of cigarettes. Tulip and Clover both sound like cows. Acacia sounds a bit like medicine. But Verbena? Hyacinth? They both could work, actually!

Although which would work *better*?

I'll think about it and decide tomorrow. During fourth-period ELA, before writing time.

Or possibly tonight, after Rania texts me back.

OPENING SENTENCE

By the next day in ELA, I still haven't answered the Hyacinth-versus-Verbena question, partly because I never heard back from Rania, so I couldn't ask her opinion.

That's the bad news.

The good news is that somehow magic happened overnight, and in my sleep I came up with an opening sentence:

> *Aster was sloshing through the Quagmire when all of a sudden she heard the shriek.*

It's perfect, right? Plops you right into the action!

I wish I could share it with everyone this minute! Read it aloud to the class, especially Ms. Bowman!

Of course, first I'll have to do a ton of explaining—who Aster is, why she's sloshing through the Quagmire, who's shrieking and why—but now that I have this incredible first sentence, I'm so excited to write it in my notebook!

And here I go!

Holding a new blue gel pen that isn't leaking, yay!

Except . . . wait, is it "shriek" or "shreik"?

It's "shriek"—I'm almost positive. *I* before *E*, except after *C*. Or when blahblahblah.

Maybe I should look it up? I mean, I *could* wait until I type it (if I ever do; I haven't decided), because then I'll have autocorrect. But the Defectors do a lot of shrieking, so I should probably get the spelling figured out before then.

Ms. Bowman has a huge print dictionary on an old-fashioned wooden stand in the back corner of the classroom, where she keeps the books she calls "free choice." She doesn't organize them in any specific way I can tell, just divides them into fiction and nonfiction—so when you want a book, you have to poke through all the titles. Which isn't a problem, at least not for me.

Before I check the dictionary, I take a minute with *The Girl Who Drank the Moon*, a book I've read three and a half times, which feels almost like a friend. Then I pick up *The Lightning Thief*, definitely one of my top ten favorites, and a book I've been planning to reread sometime soon. I'm flipping through *The City of Ember* (which I've read only once, but loved) when Ms. Bowman taps me on the shoulder.

"Lyla," she says.

I shut the book and look right into my teacher's face. How old is she? It's hard to tell. Ms. Bowman dresses in a youngish sort of way, with big, slouchy sweaters that fall off her shoulders, random bracelets on her wrist, and silver rings on most of her fingers, including her thumbs. But she has frizzy brown hair with a few gray strands at her temples, and her dark blue eyes are wrinkled in the corners. *Smile lines*, I think they're called, although I think you get them only if you're old enough.

I once heard Harrison Greller say Ms. Bowman plays bass in a rock band on weekends, although sometimes Harrison Greller just makes stuff up. On the other hand, I can almost imagine Ms. Bowman onstage. Maybe wearing Chuck Taylors and a black jumpsuit . . . ?

"You know, this is writing time," she's saying softly.

I put *The City of Ember* back on the shelf. "Sorry! I just needed to check something fast."

"No need to apologize. And actually, reading can help give you ideas."

"Oh, but I already have ideas! Like a million of them, actually."

"That's wonderful. So maybe you need a little more time to gestate?"

I swallow. "Gestate?"

"I just mean let your ideas take shape. That's also part of the writing process."

"Oh, they already have a shape! But thanks."

"Okay," she says, her eyes crinkling.

I go back to my desk, even though I haven't checked the dictionary.

Stella looks over her shoulder, scowling at me for breaking her concentration. I pretend not to notice. Sometimes Stella acts as if she's the only person in the room, and every assignment is just about getting her another A-plus. I bet she has a report-card collection back home. Maybe a shelf full of medals and trophies, too. Seriously, sometimes she reminds me of my sister.

As for Noah, his head is on the desk, like he's asleep. Again I can't help feeling sorry for him, because I can tell he'd rather be anywhere besides ELA. Even with an amazing teacher like Ms. Bowman.

I take a deep breath. And now I write in my notebook:

Aster was sloshing through the Quagmire when all of a sudden she heard the shriek.

Can you be in love with a sentence? Because that's exactly what it feels like!

Although I can't help feeling that if I write a crappy or boring or draggy second sentence, I'll ruin everything.

Okay, so maybe Ms. Bowman is right. Maybe I should gestate a little.

SUPERPOWERS

"Lyla, can I ask you a question?" Journey is eating a chicken-salad wrap that's leaking all over her plate. Too much mayo or something. Gross.

"Sure," I say. I nibble the crust off my turkey sandwich. The bread is dry and the lettuce is limp, but at least my lunch isn't gloppy like hers.

"Okay, so. If you could have any superpower in the world, which would you choose?"

Not a question I was expecting, but whatever. I think

for a second. "Probably mind reading. I think it would help me to write my characters."

Journey frowns. "What characters?"

"The ones I told you about yesterday, remember? In that book I'm writing?"

"Oh, right. The girl who flies over the swamp."

I chew my sandwich. "It's not a *swamp*, Journey, it's the Quagmire. And she doesn't fly, okay? Remember I said—"

"Right, she's not a bird or a dragon. Got it." Journey licks some mayo off her wrap. She uses her whole tongue, like she's eating an ice cream cone. I can't watch. "And you want to read her mind?"

"I just mean if I could mind-read *in real life*, it would help me know how people think. And then I could use some of that in my writing."

"Cool cool." Journey puts down her wrap which immediately falls apart. "Well, for *my* superpower I'm deciding between Prehensile Tail and Regenerative Healing. The tail thing would be awesome for combat, especially if you need to hold more than one weapon. Also it would be useful for balance, and when you're scaling a cliff. But regeneration would mean I could regrow all my missing limbs. Automatically!"

"You're missing limbs?"

"Not at the moment," she says. And then she starts humming some song I don't recognize.

I focus on my sandwich. *Maybe find another kid to eat with,* I think.

But the thing is, I've never been good at just plopping myself at someone's table. When I first started Whitman last year, I actually tried that for the first few months. *Time to make some new friends,* I told myself, because Rania was at a different school, we couldn't see each other too often, and I was sick of the kids I knew from fifth grade. And maybe I picked the wrong tables, or the wrong kids, because they all just looked at me like *Um, excuse me, Lyla, did someone say you could join us?*

Once I even tried sitting with Journey. We were in different classes for sixth grade; I didn't know much about her except that she was quiet and had incredibly long hair. But the day I sat at her table, I noticed her long hair was gone—and I was so surprised I asked what happened to it.

"Donated it." She narrowed her eyes. "Why?"

"Just curious," I said, blushing.

Then she took a huge bite of her burrito, and barely said another word. So for the rest of last year, I didn't even try talking to her again.

When I used to eat with Rania, we had tons to talk about, so much that we'd keep interrupting each other. And even when we didn't—when school was boring, or we weren't reading the same book or watching the same show—we could always just make each other laugh. But I've been at Whitman a whole year now, and I haven't found anyone like Rania. I mean, obviously I chat with people *all the time*, but I haven't found anyone to eat with every lunch period, or who I can talk to about my story. Except for Journey, even though now she's back to licking her chicken wrap.

Dahlia says I'm lucky to be in seventh grade. So either she has amnesia or she was so busy being the perfect student that she never noticed what middle school is really, actually, like.

TRESPASSING

At dismissal I have a brilliant idea: I'll head over to Emily Dickinson to see Rania, who's staying late for track-team practice the way she does most days this fall.

It's an almost-two-mile walk to her school, and the weather is chilly for late September, sunny, with a sharp wind. At least I'm wearing a heavy sweatshirt—a hand-me-down from Dahlia, soft and faded from all the washing. I usually don't like wearing Dahlia's old clothes, but this sweatshirt feels kind of perfect. Plus, it's my favorite color, kind of a purplish-grayish blue.

It takes me like thirty minutes to get there because my backpack is so heavy, thanks to my math textbook. As soon as I spot the building, I have the same reaction as always: this school is so much fancier than Whitman—newer, bigger, scarier. I'm not saying it's better, or that I'd rather go here. I actually think Whitman looks kind of cozy, full of old, dark wood and faded murals someone painted like forty million years ago: OUR ONLY PLANET. INCLUSION MEANS EVERYONE. THE FUTURE IS STEM! But compared to Dickinson our building is sort of shabby, I guess.

Also, our fields are way smaller, and they stay muddy after every rain. So I'm glad for Rania that she gets to run on Dickinson's brand-new track. Maybe if I went to this school I'd join the track team also. Who knows.

"Hey, Lyla!" someone calls.

I turn my head: it's Orion Skinner, with his new grown-up voice. Back in elementary school he sounded chirpy, like a baby bird. Although it isn't just his voice that's changed: now he's actually kind of cute—a tall, skinny Black kid with big, serious eyes.

"What are you doing here?" he asks.

I roll my eyes. "You think I'm trespassing?"

"That's not what I meant. Just—you go to Whitman now, right?"

"Yeah, I do. I love it; it's a great school." Why am I saying this? I'm not doing an ad for Whitman, and anyway, what I think isn't Orion's business. "Have you seen Rania?"

He frowns like he's trying to remember. "No. Not since Spanish."

The way he says this—his voice cracking, his eyes dropping—makes me think he might have a crush on her. Well, if he did, it wouldn't be surprising. Rania is smart and pretty and nice. Everyone always likes her, including teachers.

"Lyla? Omigod, is that you?" Suddenly she's running toward me, wearing a Chicago Cubs tee and royal blue track shorts, her long black hair in a swingy high ponytail. Rania's skin is a warm brown, so it takes a lot for her face to look red at all, but she's flushed and sweaty from track practice. "What are you doing here?" she asks, panting a little.

"I texted you last night, but you never answered. So I came to see you."

I grin as I say this, trying to ignore the fact that Orion is standing there, staring.

"You texted? When?"

"Around seven thirty." *And then again at eight,* I decide not to say.

"Oh, wait!" She grabs my sleeve. "Lyla, I'm so, so sorry! I left my charger at Ayana's, so my phone died overnight!"

"Who's Ayana?"

She laughs. "Ayana Marberry? I'm sure I told you about her. We're on track team together."

"Oh, right," I say, even though I'm pretty sure she never mentioned any Ayana before right now.

"Anyway. Are you okay, Ly? Did something happen?"

"No, everything's fine. I just wanted to see you."

"Well, I'm glad you came over! Even if I'm a sweaty mess." She laughs. Rania has the best laugh, bright and sparkly. I suddenly think how much I miss hearing it all the time.

"Can you wait around a sec?" she asks. "Practice just ended and I desperately need to change."

"Sure," I say as Rania runs indoors. By now my backpack is killing my shoulders, so I take it off as I lean against a stone wall.

For some reason, Orion is still standing there with his hands in his pockets. I glance at him like, *Excuse me, are you waiting for something?* He coughs into his elbow and walks away.

Then I take out my phone. Hardly anyone besides Rania

and my mom ever texts me, but I check anyway, for something to do.

A few minutes later, Rania comes outside in her regular clothes, walking with two girls she introduces as Ayana and Gracie. Ayana is a tiny Black girl with purple glasses and short natural hair. Gracie is white, tall and thin, with braces and long reddish hair. And the three of them—I mean including Rania—are all laughing about something that happened during track practice.

"Yeah, and when Mr. Verplanck blew the whistle—" Gracie is saying.

"He's our coach," Rania explains, smiling at me.

"—omigod, I almost peed my pants!"

"No you didn't, Gracie," Ayana tells her, giggling.

"How do you know?" Gracie's laugh is so loud I bet you can hear it over at Whitman. "I swear, when he said *one more lap*—"

"He can't say his *l*'s, so it sounds like 'yap,'" Ayana explains to me.

Gracie hoots. *"One more yap,"* she repeats.

"Lyla doesn't want to hear about practice," Rania tells them.

"No, no, it's fine," I say, although I'd never make fun of

how someone speaks. *And neither would Rania,* I tell myself. Even though she doesn't tell them to stop.

After that it sort of is fine, really, as the four of us walk into town. But I don't say much, because mostly they're talking about kids I don't know, or stuff that happened during track practice.

And of course now I can't tell Rania about my story. Because if I tell her the first sentence, and explain why I'm having trouble with the second one, maybe Ayana and Gracie will think it's funny. And talk about me to other kids at Dickinson, and almost pee their pants.

MEANINGFUL EXPERIENCE

When I get home, I can hear loud voices coming from Dahlia's room.

"Mom, this isn't helping."

"Well, what *would* help, then? What do you need from me?"

"I need you to leave me alone!"

"Yes, sweetheart, but that's exactly what I've been doing, and nothing's getting done! And didn't your school counselor say seniors were supposed to have a rough draft by the end of the summer? It's already the end of September!"

"Mom, I can read the calendar, okay?"

"Don't use that voice with me, Dahlia."

"Fine! Whose voice should I use?"

I really don't want to hear this argument, but it's not like I have a choice. Dahlia's bedroom is right down the hall from mine, and the walls are thin. Also, her door is wide open.

When my mom and my sister go quiet for a few seconds, I hope the arguing is over. But then I hear Mom asking Dahlia for "that sheet they gave us at the meeting."

"What sheet? What meeting?"

"The college-prep meeting, Dahlia. At the end of last year, remember? With suggested topics for the essay."

"Arrgghh. Fine, I'll look for it, all right?"

I hear my sister's desk drawer opening and slamming shut. A stack of papers thudding on a desk. A swivel chair squeaking.

"Here. Okay, Mom? Are you happy?"

"You know, I'm doing my best to ignore that tone, but you're really pushing it, Dahlia." (Pause—sound of papers shuffling.) "This is how you kept all your college stuff? It's so disorganized!"

"Because I've been focusing on my classes! Isn't that supposed to be my priority?"

"Well, yes, of course, but you had all summer—"

"When did I have any time this summer? I had to work at that horrible day camp every day! And at the food bank on weekends!"

"Calm down, please! Maybe you can write about your food-bank experience."

"Are you serious?"

"Excuse me?"

"Mom, the food bank wasn't 'an experience'! And it wasn't about *me*. Those people were hungry! I was just there to put out food!"

"Yes, but one of the topics they suggest is A Meaningful Experience. So all I'm suggesting—"

"You're not suggesting, Mom! You're forcing me!"

I can't listen to this anymore, so I stick in my earbuds. But a few minutes later I hear my sister's door slam shut. And then I hear Mom banging pots on the kitchen counter like she's making supper now, but furiously.

CONTEST

The next day at the start of ELA, Ms. Bowman has an announcement

"Listen up, dust bunnies," she says, smiling.

One of my favorite things about Ms. Bowman: she never calls us "boys and girls" or "folks" or "people." It's like every day she invents a whole new name for us: Gumdrops. Cats and kittens. Tiddlywinks. Peas and carrots. Firecrackers. And even though "dust bunnies" is kind of a strange name to call your students, it makes me smile.

"Okay," she says when everyone finally settles. "So the

town library board has just announced the dates for their annual Young Writers Contest. If any of you are interested, you can submit a poem, a short story, or a nonfiction piece up to ten pages long, but you need to get it to the library by November first."

"Is there a prize?" Stella asks, because of course that's all she cares about.

"Yep, there is. First prize is two hundred dollars, second prize is one hundred dollars, and third prize is fifty. They usually award a few honorable mentions, too—no cash, but it's still nice recognition. Although in my opinion, the best reason to enter is a chance to share your work."

"Can we submit more than one thing?" Stella asks.

"You can, but the limit is three submissions per student."

"What if we don't want to enter anything?" Noah asks.

"Totally fine," Ms. Bowman says, pressing her palms together. "This contest is *completely optional*, okay? But since you dust bunnies are working on stories in this class, maybe some of you will consider submitting. Or not. Up to you."

She seems eager to switch topics, because she starts talking about our reading groups, and when we're choosing the next books to discuss.

But I can't stop thinking about this contest. When

Dahlia was in middle school, she entered a poem called "Clouds" and won second prize. Our family went to a ceremony at the library where all the winners read their entries aloud, and had their photo in the local newspaper and on the town website. And when someone asked Dahlia what she was going to do with her prize money, she answered, "Donate it to the SPCA." So that got in the newspaper too: how this kid wasn't only a great poet, but also an animal lover and "model citizen."

And seriously, it's not like I ever compete with my sister, because of course there's no point. Everyone knows Dahlia Benjamin is a superstar, incredible at everything she does: math, science, art, softball, flute, poetry. Even citizenship.

Last year it didn't even occur to me to submit one of my exactly-five-paragraph essays. But now the thought of entering my story and getting first prize takes over my brain. And when it's time to work on our stories, I flip to the back page of my notebook. I write *Aster and Hyacinth*, *Aster and Verbena*. Over and over, like somehow seeing those names in my own handwriting, written in my favorite, friendly blue gel pen, will help me decide.

Until Ms. Bowman tells us to leave our writing notebooks on her desk, and it's time for lunch.

THE SECOND SENTENCE

 ster was sloshing through the Quagmire when all of a sudden she heard the shriek.

I'm staring at my writing notebook in ELA. We've been writing our stories for four days now, and all I have is this one perfect sentence. I still love it, of course, but I'm starting to panic a little. Because I definitely should have more words by now, shouldn't I?

Although *which* words? You can't just have a dramatic opening sentence and an okay second one; you need a dramatic opening *chapter*. It needs to grab the reader and yell, KEEP READING—especially if the reader is judging a creative-writing contest! And the thing is, I keep coming up with more sentences, enough to fill a paragraph, or a page . . . but every time I write them, and read them over, I decide they're horrible.

Like this one:

> *Aster was sloshing through the Quagmire when all of a sudden she heard the shriek. Could it be one of the Defectors? She knew they haunted the Quagmire but before today she'd never heard any because she lived with her parents and her beautiful older sister Verbena/Hyacinth in a small cottage in the kingdom of . . .*

Nope. Too draggy. And off-topic.
Or like this:

> *Aster was sloshing through the Quagmire when all of a sudden she heard the shriek. Right away she knew what it was, because she'd heard about it from her tutor, the Seer, who told her the story of the Defectors, the barefoot red-eyed creatures with black capes and shaved heads who were cursed*

to haunt the dark, dangerous swamp along with the
one-toed Beast . . .

Also nope. Too long and describe-y. Plus it sounds like a horror story, which this isn't. Even though there's also going to be a bunch of witches.

Aster was sloshing through the Quagmire when all
of a sudden she heard the shriek. It was a very
loud, high-pitched sound . . .

Well, obviously. Because who doesn't know the meaning of "shriek"?

So I just keep writing and crossing out, writing and crossing out, and now the page is totally unreadable, even by me.

I decide to take action: I'll rip out the page and just start over!

But.

When you tear out a page from a spiral notebook, it leaves shreddy bits in the spirals, which I poke out with my pen. And of course you can't just leave a heap of shreddy bits all over your desk, so I get up to toss them in the garbage can.

Then I rewrite my first sentence—slowly, in my best

handwriting: *Aster was sloshing through the Quagmire when all of a sudden—*

My hand is sweating, smudging the blue ink. Should I switch to pencil? Maybe I should, because at least then I could erase!

Except pencils aren't friendly like blue gel pens. Plus the lead (if it's even real lead) can get smudgy too, and also if you don't press hard enough, it fades. Ms. Kobrin makes us use pencil in math class, and I can barely read my notes from two weeks ago.

Yeah, definitely keeping the blue gel pen!

All right, now you need to focus, Lyla: all of a sudden *what?*

Good question.

Maybe I should do a flashback so you understand *why* Aster's in the Quagmire, and who's doing the shrieking. (Or shreiking. I still need to look that up.) Although can you have a flashback after just one sentence? It does seem kind of soon. And I don't think I've ever read a book that begins: *Here we are in the present! Boom! Now we're in the past!*

Or possibly I could start in the past and then flash forward. Or switch back and forth. That could be sort of cool, right? Except all the back-and-forth could get tricky to follow.

Although if I used different colored ink for different time periods . . . ?

No, no, too complicated.

Maybe I should give myself more time to gestate! Ms. Bowman said it's part of the writing process, didn't she? And I'm sure it's better to write too little instead of too much.

Not like Stella, who obviously thinks the more words she writes, the higher her grade—as if Ms. Bowman is the kind of teacher who just counts paragraphs, like Mr. Delgado. Or maybe Stella thinks if she writes three stories she can submit all three, and triple her chances of winning the writing contest.

I wonder if they just give you a check if you win. Because I bet Stella would rather have a trophy for her bookshelf. To go with all her other trophies and report cards.

Did Dahlia get a trophy when her poem won second prize? I try to remember. Maybe you only get one if you win first.

I wonder if they engrave your name—

Suddenly there's a hand on my shoulder. "How's it going, Lyla?" Ms. Bowman is asking.

"Great," I say as my stomach flips over like a pancake.

"Are you writing?" She's asking in a friendly, quiet voice, but I can't tell if anyone can hear.

"Sort of."

"I don't see your pen moving."

"I'm actually gestating first. In my head."

Idiot, I yell at myself. *Where else would you be gestating, except in your head?*

"Yes, pre-writing can be helpful," Ms. Bowman says, nodding a little. "But you know, Lyla, at a certain point it's good to jump in with both feet. I always find that ideas come as you're working. You really don't have to have it all figured out before you begin."

"Oh, I know that! I already have most of it figured out, though. I'm just deciding a few things."

She crinkles her eyes at me. "Sounds good," she says. "Well, let me know if you'd ever like to chat about your story. I'm always available, you know."

I watch as she walks over to Noah, hunched over his desk like he's asleep, probably dreaming of numbers instead of words.

THE SECRET

When I get home that afternoon, Dahlia is in the living room playing a video game called *BeforeTimes VI*. This is weird because usually after school she goes straight to her room, like she can't wait to start her calculus homework.

I squish between my sister and Spumoni (who's taking over two thirds of the sofa), watching her blast some sort of pterodactylish creature with fiery orange eyes and a glowing red chest.

"Who's that again?" I ask.

"Shh, Lyla, I'm concentrating," Dahlia says, not taking her eyes off the screen.

About ten minutes later she defeats the creature. By that I mean one of the blasts turns him into vacuum-cleaner dust.

"Victory at last." Dahlia stands and stretches. "What time is it?"

I check my phone. "Three fifty-seven. Why are you asking? Where's your phone?"

"On my desk. People wouldn't stop texting, and it was stressing me out, so I left it uncharged last night. And I'm just about ready to throw it in the garbage."

"Seriously?" I say. Because my sister is the kind of person who takes her phone into the bathroom. Sleeps with it under her pillow, probably. I don't know why she's on her phone so much, but I do know that she spends a lot of time texting her best friend, Sophie, and also this boy named Nico. He's either Dahlia's friend or more-than-friend; whenever I ask, she just shrugs and smiles.

Dahlia plops back down on the sofa like suddenly all her energy is vacuum-cleaner dust. "So how was your school day?"

This question surprises me. Only parents ever ask about your "school day."

"Fine, I guess," I say. "I really like Ms. Bowman. She's the opposite of Mr. Delgado."

"Yeah, Ms. Bowman's great. Did you know she plays bass in a band?"

"That's what I heard from a kid in my class. But it sounded fake."

"Oh, it's true. Sophie saw her band at a farmers market once. She said they rocked."

"A farmers market?" I try to imagine Ms. Bowman playing bass in front of people selling homemade jam and fancy lettuce, but it's not easy.

"Or was it a flea market?" Dahlia combs her perfect hair with her fingers. "Some kind of market, anyway; I don't remember."

"Huh." For some reason, then I blurt: "Anyway, I'm sort of having trouble in her class. Writing my story, I mean."

Why am I telling her this? Maybe because Dahlia is acting like Not Dahlia.

My sister stops finger-combing and raises her eyebrows. "What do you mean by 'having trouble'?"

"I just can't get started! I really, really want it to be good—but I've been thinking about it so long it's like I have the whole thing in my head, all knotted up. And I can't untangle it to find the beginning."

"Oh yeah, beginnings are rough." She rubs Spumoni's ears while he yawns smelly dog breath all over us. "So maybe forget about the beginning and just start somewhere in the middle."

"What do you mean?"

"I mean, there's no law you have to start writing a story on page one, right? What if you started with page twenty-five and worked your way back to the beginning? It's what I do sometimes when I'm writing a long essay: I write out all my arguments, and all my evidence, and then, once I know what I'm arguing, I do the intro and the conclusion."

"Huh, maybe," I say. But I'm thinking: *Yeah, that method might work for a US history paper, but not if you're writing a whole novel. Because don't you need to tell the story to learn stuff about your characters? That's what Ms. Bowman said, anyway.*

The other thing I'm thinking: *If I'm entering my book in the writing contest, I can't just submit whatever's on page twenty-five! I have to submit the first ten pages or the judges won't understand what they're even reading.*

But I don't say this to Dahlia, because I don't want her knowing I'm entering a contest she already won. Even if she won for poetry, and just second prize.

Although Dahlia is being so nice, so calm, so *Not Dahlia*, that I can't stop myself from talking. "Anyhow, maybe that will work for you, too," I say.

My sister blinks at me. "Maybe *what* will work? What are you talking about?"

"I mean with your college essay. What if you started writing it from the middle. Like you just said."

My sister's eyes shrink. "Okay, Lyla, *first* of all, the problem with my college essay isn't that I can't *begin*. It's that I have *nothing to say*. Nothing I *want* to say."

"You? But Dahlia, you're so—"

"And how do you even know about my college essay?"

"I heard you and Mom fighting yesterday."

"Oh, right." She grits her teeth. "Yeah, I guess we did get kind of loud. Sorry."

"It's okay. I'm sorry you're having trouble. I mean with Mom, and everything."

"Thanks." Now Dahlia's face puckers and gets all pink. For a second I think she's going to cry. But she doesn't. "Ly, can I tell you a secret? But only if you promise not to tell Mom. Or Dad, either."

"Sure. Of course."

"Okay. I'm not going to college."

I gasp. *"What?"*

"Yeah. I'm just so tired of being stressed, you know? At school all anyone talks about is where you're applying, and who else is applying there, and what their GPA is like, and did you visit the campus, and did you fill out the financial aid form yet? The whole thing is destroying my stomach, and I haven't slept in like a week. Two weeks, actually. *And* I'm convinced it's a huge waste of money."

I stare at my sister. "So what will you do instead? Of college, I mean."

"No idea." She hugs a sofa pillow in front of her belly like it's a shield. "Maybe work with animals? Or travel? I really don't know, Lyla. Anything."

I can barely talk. "When . . . did you decide this?"

"Today. Last night, actually, when I couldn't sleep. And this morning, I knew it was right." She grabs my wrist and squeezes hard. "You'd better not say anything to Mom, because she'll totally freak."

"I said I wouldn't, Dahlia! But you're going to have to tell her *sometime*, right?"

"Theoretically," my sister says as we hear the front door opening, and Mom announcing that she needs help with the groceries.

EARBUDS

So you mean you've been playing video games all after-noon?"

"Ugh, Mom, what do you want from me?"

"Just for you to do your best! And not make this into a daily struggle!"

"You're the one making it a struggle!"

"Dahlia, please just stop, okay? All I want—"

"—is to do the applications for me, right? And the essay! And maybe go to college . . ."

Uh-oh, here they go again.

I can't listen. Especially after what Dahlia just told me.

Why doesn't she tell Mom the not-going-to-college stuff and get it over with? Otherwise they're just going to keep on fighting like this, over and over, every single day. And Dahlia is already stressed out, so how is fighting with Mom helping?

"Dahlia, why are you acting like this?"

"Because you're driving me crazy! Why can't you leave me alone?"

"Why? Because Dad and I love you, and we don't want you to sell yourself short! After all the work you've done to get to this point—"

"You think the whole point of going to school and studying hard is just to get me into a fancy college? What for? So you can brag to all your friends?"

"I'll pretend you didn't say that. Look, we only want the best for you, Dahlia. I know you're under a lot of stress—"

"Yes, I am, and you're making it worse!"

"All right, so why don't you let me help—"

I stick in my earbuds. I'm not even listening to music or anything; I just need to stop overhearing Dahlia and Mom. Because it's like: before today it was awful hearing them fight, but now that Dahlia told me her plan (if you can call it a plan, since she doesn't know what she wants to do), it's practically torture.

And with all the yelling downstairs, forget about math homework. Even with earbuds, I can't focus on exponents.

Instead I text Rania.

HEY.

This time she replies right away: HEY LYLA. I was just about to text you!!

Me: Really??? That's so funny! What's up?

Rania: Nothing, just boring Spanish homework!! I hate irregular verbs!! But can you come this weekend for a sleepover??

Me: YES DEFINITELY!!! First I need to ask Mom but I'm sure she'll let me.

Rania: Yaayyyy!!! Can you be here at 5 on Sat? We'll make pizza!!!

Okay, I tell myself, *so at least here's one great thing to look forward to. And perfect timing: I won't have to be home to hear more fighting!*

Now as I take out my math textbook, I'm grinning. And for the next hour I zone out on exponents, and don't think about my story even once.

FAMILY TREE

Friday drags along like a turtle poking its way through sludge. But in ELA I do add a teeny bit to my story:

Aster was sloshing through The Quagmire when all of a sudden she heard the shriek.

She recognized it right away. The Seer had warned her about it before: "First you hear the shriek, then the Defectors attack!" So she knew she needed to run really fast.

I read it over like seven times. Not draggy or obvious or off-topic or describe-y! Except "she needed to run really fast" sounds terrible. I try to think of a better way to put it, but everything I come up with—*run like lightning, run like the wind, run like an antelope*—is such a cliché. And maybe you can get away with a cliché on page fifty, but on page one? You absolutely can't.

I cross out the last sentence.

Aster was sloshing through the Quagmire when—

Ugh. Ugh-ugh-ugh-ugh.

My hand can't even write this sentence anymore. My eyes refuse to read it. It's like I've fallen out of love with it somehow. How did this happen?

Maybe the problem is starting with Aster, and the sloshing, and the shrieking. I mean, just because I had the *idea* that this is a perfect way to begin doesn't mean it is! What if this scene is just too dramatic for an opening chapter? And the whole reason I keep stalling out?

Now it hits me: I'm doing this story completely wrong! I should forget about Aster in the Quagmire, and switch focus to the big sister, Verbena/Hyacinth! Because really, you won't care that Aster is saving her if you think she's just this boring Perfect Princess, right? And so far the only thing I've decided about Aster's sister is that she studies hard and cares about personal hygiene! Which is boring, boring, boring.

I'm breaking out in a sweat. It's like I'm turning liquid— my face, my neck, my armpits, my hands. Especially my hands. It's hard to grip my pen, and now the paper is getting wrinkly. And smeary.

All right, I need to try to CALM DOWN.

Because this is not too late to fix! I can just start over, can't I?

So what if I switched the opening to something like: *Verbena/Hyacinth was brushing her long, perfect hair as she gazed out the window—*

Bleh. Even worse, and a bazillion times more boring!

If I picked up this book, I'd stop reading immediately!

Verbena/Hyacinth needs some action! Also a backstory!

Such as?

Okay, so what if she's not as perfect as I thought? What if she actually fights a little with her parents? And maybe with Aster, too. Because no one is the Perfect Princess all the time, right? And you can't write a story with zero conflict!

Also, I need to think harder about the parents. What

do I know about them? Just that they're poor, which is why getting chosen for Vanguard matters so much. But they're royalty, so that means they come from a long dynasty. How do you get to be (a) royalty and (b) poor? Maybe they got disowned for marrying the wrong person or something. And it turned into a kind of war with the rest of the family!

Ooh, I like that, actually. It's romantic. And dramatic! And will make the parents un-boring too.

Although I should probably map out the whole family tree, so I don't lose track of anybody, including the relatives they're still at war with. Which means a whole lot of not-main-but-still-important characters.

I open to a new page and start drawing a family tree. The branches spread onto the next page, and the page after that.

Technically I'm not writing my story, but at least Ms. Bowman sees me moving my pen. When the bell rings, she actually winks at me and calls out, "Have a good weekend, Lyla," and I call back, "You too, Ms. Bowman!"

Although it comes out a little too loud, and Noah looks at me funny.

AXOLOTL

Lunch is the regular. I have a bowl of turkey chili and Journey has a gooey panini, with melted cheese oozing out the sides whenever she takes a bite. (Melted cheese is one of those foods that's amazing when it's yours, but kind of disgusting when it isn't, so I try not to look.) She's talking about her axolotl named Penelope, how last night they fed her raw chicken instead of night crawlers.

"Um, a little gross for lunch conversation?" I say, keeping my eyes off her drippy cheese.

Journey shrugs and keeps talking. "Basically the rule

for axolotls is that they're carnivores, so you shouldn't give them plant stuff. Also, you feed them only once every two or three days."

"'Kay, got it," I say, like I'm taking notes for axolotl-sitting.

All of a sudden, then, her eyes light up. "Hey, Lyla. Want to come over tomorrow? You can meet all my pets, not just Penelope."

"Tomorrow? Sorry, can't," I say quickly. "I have a sleepover with my best friend Rania, so."

"You mean at night?"

"Well, yeah, obviously. You don't do sleepovers in the afternoon."

"So come for breakfast! Penelope is a morning person anyway. And so is Albert."

"Albert?"

"Lyla, I told you. Did you forget?" She rolls her eyes. "My bearded dragon?"

Bearded dragon. It almost sounds like a creature in my story. And I've never seen one in real life, so meeting Albert—and Journey's other pets too—could be sort of fun, really. Besides, I tell myself, if I go over to Journey's house, it'll take care of Saturday morning. In the late afternoon I'll go over to Rania's, so I'll have almost an entire day away from home and all the yelling about college essays.

"Sure, I'll come over," I tell Journey, who doesn't stop grinning as she tucks her bangs into the brim of her cap.

That night I'm thinking we're actually having a calm dinner with zero fighting, when Dad ruins everything by asking Dahlia what she has planned for the weekend.

"Not much," Dahlia says with a mouth full of mashed potato. "Why?"

Dad and Mom exchange a look. She nods at him like, *Your turn.*

Dad clears his throat. "Well, baby. Don't you think it might be a good idea to get that college essay going? As long as nothing else is happening this weekend?"

"Yeah, maybe," Dahlia says. "Lyla, can you please pass the salt?"

I pass the salt.

We all watch as Dahlia shakes a blizzard of salt on her potatoes.

Then Mom says, "You know, Dahlia, I was talking to my friend Lisa the other day. She mentioned this guy people hire to help kids with their essays. His name is Daniel Chen; he used to work in college admissions. And he's very nice, she says. He comes right to your house—"

"*Wait.*" Dahlia's eyes are bugging. "*Mom.* You want to

hire some rando to write my essay for me? Isn't that illegal?"

"Not 'some rando,' and not to write it *for* you." The way Dad says this, you can tell he's already discussed it with Mom. "Just to help you *with* it. Maybe brainstorm a little—"

"*No.*" Dahlia puts down her fork. "No *thank* you."

"Dahlia—"

"It's supposed to be my essay. *My* essay, Dad! And I wish everyone would please back off and let me do it on my own! Please!"

"Sure." Mom's mouth is tight. "As long as you're aware of the deadlines. And don't keep procrastinating."

Dahlia jabs her fork in her potatoes. Her face is red.

If she's really not going to college, why doesn't she just tell them right now, and get it over with? What's stopping her?

I try to catch my sister's eye, but she's too busy murdering her mashed potatoes.

The table goes quiet.

The weird thing is how the quiet feels worse than the fighting.

And how come Mom and Dad aren't asking about my weekend plans too? All they ever think about is Dahlia, Dahlia, Dahlia.

Did it used to be like this before all the applying-to-college stuff?

63

Not really. Although Mom did make me wear Dahlia's old clothes sometimes when I wanted new ones I picked out myself. And even though they didn't exactly compare how we did in school, they always did make a giant fuss over Dahlia's report cards.

But lately it's like I'm not even here. Like they don't notice I am, I mean.

"By the way, I'm going to Journey's house tomorrow for breakfast," I announce loudly. "She wants to show me her axolotl."

"Her what?" Dad says.

"You know. Those cute, tiny salamanders with pink gills and a big smile—"

"Oooh, I love them, they're so *adorable*," Dahlia says. All of a sudden her face lights up and her voice sounds hyper-enthusiastic, although I'm guessing that's mostly about the change of subject.

"Yeah," I say. "Journey's axolotl is named Penelope. And she has a bunch of other pets—"

"Journey?" Mom says. Her forehead scrunches. "Do I know her mom?"

I shrug. "Maybe. I don't know; I never met her."

"And didn't you ask me about going to Rania's tomorrow?"

Okay, so she was paying attention after all. "Yes, but for a sleepover. This is in the morning. For breakfast."

"Busy social life," Dad says, throwing me a smile as he slices his chicken.

"Yeah, I guess," I say.

Dahlia pushes away her plate and groans. "Oh, Lyla," she says. "Can we please, please trade places? I'd *so* much rather be you."

"Uh-huh," I say, not even knowing what that means.

ANIMALS

I'm not sure what I expected from Journey's house, but it isn't this.

Journey's house looks totally normal on the outside. A medium-sized gray-shingled house with a red door. Yellow and purple chrysanthemums in planters on the steps. A huge oak tree with a tire swing in the front yard.

Why is this so shocking? Did I think she'd live in a yurt? Or a houseboat? Or maybe a lab, or a wildlife sanctuary?

I ring the doorbell. It makes a Mozart-sounding melody, and right away Journey opens the door, like she's been standing there, waiting. She's dressed in shorts and a NASA tee, even though it's chilly out today. No newsboy cap, though, so I can see her almost-blond hair is getting longer, fuller, like she could actually use a haircut.

Wow, she's lucky her hair grows so fast. I wish mine did.

"Hey, you made it," she says, grinning.

"Yeah, but I've never been on this street before, so I had to check a map." Does that sound a little rude? I think maybe it does, so I add, "Thanks for inviting me."

"No problem."

I can't help thinking this is a funny thing to say. I mean, if someone thanks you for inviting them, you answer with something like, "I'm glad you could come." Because who said coming here was a *problem*? Not me.

She leads me down the hall to her kitchen, which is messy in a cozy sort of way: dishes in the sink, a few crumbs on the white counters, notes on the fridge in a grown-up's handwriting. *Don't forget to check expiration dates! Load the dishwasher, please!*

The parent-ness of these notes is another surprise. Because what did I think—that Journey lived alone with her animals like Pippi Longstocking?

"Want a corn muffin?" Journey points to a tray of muffins with slightly burnt tops. "My mom just took them out of the oven. I think they're still warm."

So this is our breakfast, obviously. I choose one of the slightly burnt ones to be polite, and take a bite off the top. The muffin falls apart in my hand; I ask for a napkin to catch the crumbs.

She opens a drawer and hands me a cloth one, like they use in restaurants. Which is actually the first weird thing that's happened since I got here.

"This muffin is really good," I say. "Aren't you having one?"

She does a gesture like she's tugging on the brim of an invisible cap. "No, I ate breakfast already. I wasn't sure if . . ." She looks away.

Wasn't sure if what? If I'd show up? Suddenly I feel a teeny bit guilty.

"Well, you should definitely have one later," I tell her. "This is like the best corn muffin ever."

Journey smiles. "I'll tell Mom you said that."

"Isn't she home? Your mom, I mean."

"Yeah, she's in the shower. She just got off the treadmill."

"My mom does the treadmill too! Especially on weekends."

Journey squints like I've said something dumb. Which, okay, maybe I did. Like: *Ooh, our moms have something in common!*

"Hey, want to meet Penelope?" she asks.

"Now? Oh, okay." I rest the barely eaten muffin on the napkin, which I leave on the counter.

Journey leads me up the big winding staircase to a small, dark room that smells a little spicy. Sort of the way some kids smell after PE—but also different in a way I can't explain.

"So this is my animal room," Journey says. "I don't like the word 'pet,' so I say 'animal' instead."

"What's wrong with 'pet'?"

"It's not respectful."

"Huh," I say. "Okay."

"Want to meet Ray-anne?"

"Who?"

"My hamster," Journey says a bit impatiently. "I'm sure I told you, Lyla."

"Sorry. You have so many . . . *animals*, it's hard to keep track. Why is she called that?"

"You don't like the name Ray-anne?"

"Ray-anne is great. I'm just really interested in names! Like for my story."

"You mean the one about the Quagmire?"

"Yeah, that one," I say. "Although my story isn't *about* the Quagmire. And I still need names for some of the characters. How do you decide what to call your animals?"

"Well, I guess I don't really *decide*. I think it's more like you have to live with them awhile, and then they just sort of tell you. If you're listening."

I think about that a second. Is it possible to listen to your characters, too? I mean, if you're the one who wrote them?

"So where's Penelope?" I say the name of her axolotl so Journey knows I remember.

"Come over here so you can meet her."

I follow Journey to the corner of the room. Under a curtained window is a large tank with a sandy bottom, a few sharp rocks, a purple plastic cave, and several plants that look wavy, like ferns. At first I don't see anyone in the tank; but when Journey taps the glass, I spot a tiny pinkish creature with bright red gills and black eyes. Suddenly it's swimming toward her finger. And smiling. Or seems to be.

"Omigod, she's so cute," I say, gushing like my sister.

"Isn't she?" Journey beams proudly. "Although she's still a baby. I read an article: apparently axolotls can grow to a foot long."

"Whoa."

"Yeah, there's a lot I'm still learning about her. And I was thinking about what you said the other day, how you wished your superpower was reading minds. What I really wish is that I could read Penelope's."

I almost laugh. "Read her *mind*? But Journey—"

"Yeah, I know: Penelope's mind is not like a human's! But she has her own axolotl way of thinking, right? And wouldn't it be cool to go inside her world?"

I nod. Because I know it's not what Journey's talking about, but *going inside Penelope's world* sounds a bit like writing her story, in a way. If you take out all the words, I mean.

Journey lowers her voice. "Can I tell you a secret, Lyla? Next I'm saving up for a sugar glider."

"A *what*?"

"Shh." She frowns at me. "You know, those tiny, furry creatures with huge eyes! They're nocturnal, but during the day you carry them around in little pouches. Wouldn't that be amazing? Although first I need to convince my parents."

Journey starts humming a song I don't recognize as she feeds a defrosted mouse to Percy, the corn snake. I watch from a few feet away, because I'm not in love with snakes. Or with mice, frosted or defrosted.

And I have this thought: *It's almost like Journey has superpowers when it comes to animals. Like she just* gets *them, even if she can't read their minds.*

How do you do that?

All of a sudden Journey gasps. "Argh, Lyla, I forgot to introduce you to Albert! He has excellent manners; he'll be furious with me!"

OFF BALANCE

I stay at Journey's house much longer than I planned. I'm not sure how it happens, except after hanging out in the animal room, we end up in the backyard, where Journey and her dad are building a new hutch for her rabbits, Primrose and Strawberry. We cuddle the rabbits for a bit, she shows me her hummingbird feeder and her butterfly garden—and then we realize we're both starving for lunch, so her mom orders us a pizza.

It takes about an hour to be delivered. By the time I leave, it's almost three o'clock.

"I hope you'll come back soon, Lyla," Journey's mom says at the door. She grasps my hand like this is how you say goodbye to kids. "Maybe next weekend?"

Journey looks horrified. "Mom, Lyla has other stuff to do."

I almost protest that I'm not that busy, actually—but to be honest, it would be weird to accept an invitation from someone's mom. And anyway, I need to reserve weekends for Rania. Who's waiting for me right now, I remind myself.

So I pull my hand away, thank them for the pizza and the corn muffin, and race home to pack my backpack for the sleepover.

About an hour later, I'm at Rania's. Her younger brother, Rohan, answers the door; he's staring at his Switch, not even looking at me as he hollers, "Hey, Lyla's here!" and immediately disappears.

But I've been at this house so many times over the last few years that it's not like I need someone to show me around. I walk past the kitchen, where Rania's mom waves hello as she talks on her phone.

"Go ahead—they're all in her room," she tells me. Right away she continues her phone call, so I don't interrupt to ask who she means by *they*. And *all*.

My stomach twists a little as I climb the stairs to

Rania's room and knock on her semi-closed door.

"Yay, it's Lyla!" Rania shouts immediately. "What took you so long?"

"Sorry, I had something else to do." I'm not sure why I don't mention Journey, but I don't.

Rania throws her arms around me. She's a big hugger; you'd think I'd expect it by now, but I still have to take a step, off balance.

As soon as she unblocks the doorway I see Ayana and Gracie sitting cross-legged on her bed. Also another girl I've never seen before. She has thick dark hair that falls in her face in a way you can tell is on purpose.

My mouth goes dry.

How come I thought it would be just the two of us? Did Rania ever say it would be? I can't remember.

Do I even want to stay? Maybe it's not too late to go home.

Oh, Lyla. Don't be such a baby.

"Lyla, you already know Ayana and Gracie, and this is Maeve," Rania is saying. "We're in all the same classes, plus track. Poor me, haha! And Maeve, this is Lyla. Who I met in first grade!"

"That's so funny," Maeve says. Her voice is husky, with a hidden laugh. "I don't remember *anything* about first grade. Not even my teacher's name."

"Well, Lyla and I had Ms. Krakauer." Rania grins. "She had a missing tooth and a big hairy mole on her cheek."

"Eww, she sounds like a witch," Gracie says.

"You mean because she had a mole? That's such a cliché." I look at Rania. "Anyway, she was really nice. She always let us sit together, remember?"

"Of *course* I remember," Rania says. "You were always drawing comics with speech balloons! And I was jealous because I could barely write. Or draw."

"But *you* were always great at math. Even in first grade."

Gracie types something into her phone. Ayana bites her pinkie nail. It's obvious they don't want to hear about first grade.

"Lyla goes to Whitman now," Rania tells Maeve.

Maeve pushes her hair out of her eyes. "Seriously? My condolences."

"What for?" I ask.

"Nothing. Just that it's old and depressing. And that track's a *mess*."

"Well, lucky for me I don't do track."

Maeve cocks her head. "Oh no? What *do* you do, then?"

I can't explain my answer. It's like the words just fly out of my mouth.

"I'm a writer," I answer. "I'm writing a fantasy novel."

PRESTIGIOUS

Of course, you can't just announce you're writing a novel without explaining something about the plot. So I tell them about Aster and Verbena (if that's her name). And how when Aster finds out about Vanguard, she has to cross the Quagmire to save her sister, which means dealing with the witches and battling the one-toed Beast. Also the Defectors.

Maybe I'm going into too much detail about the shrieking, though, because I notice Ayana giving Gracie a look, and Maeve picking a scab on her arm.

"Anyway, that's the main idea of the story," I say. "Although there's a ton more to the plot! I may even make it into a series."

"Whoa, a series," Ayana says. "That's so much writing."

"Yes, but it's what I love to do most. The thing I'm best at, so." I shrug.

Maeve cough-laughs into her hair.

"Can I ask you something, Lyla?" Gracie says. "What's a quagmire?"

"Basically a swamp," I say.

"So why didn't you just call it that?"

"Oh, because quagmire is a fancier word," Maeve says, rolling her eyes at Gracie.

I swallow. *Why* didn't *I call it the Swamp? Should I change it?*

No. Quagmire is better. I don't know why, but it just is.

What does Maeve know, anyway?

"Hey Lyla, I just thought of something," Rania says. "You should enter that writing contest at the library! I heard Orion talking about it a few days ago."

"Yeah, he would," Maeve says.

I look at Maeve. "What does that mean?"

"Nothing. Just that it's the sort of thing he'd do."

"Because he likes to write?"

"No, because he's kind of a geek."

"Well, *I* think he's very nice. And smart," Rania protests, although not very hard. Then she throws me a look like, *Uh, maybe time to change the subject, okay?*

But now I can't shut up. Won't shut up. "Yeah, our ELA teacher told us about that writing contest a few days ago. I'm definitely submitting my book, at least the opening chapters. The first three winners get prize money, and there's this whole big ceremony at the library, where you read your stuff aloud. And if Orion enters too, great. It's extremely prestigious."

Prestigious? Why did I say that? Where did that word even come from? Who cares about prestigious?

Everyone is staring at me now.

"Oookaaay," Maeve says.

"Well, good luck, Lyla," Ayana says brightly. "I hope you win *all* the prize money."

"And beat Orion," Gracie adds. For some reason, then, the two of them start giggling.

I glance at Rania. She's sending another message with her eyes, and it's not too hard to guess what it is.

❋ ❋ ❋

After that it's like I don't trust myself to talk. I barely say a word the whole time we're making pizza, and also when we're watching *Greenhouse Academy*. Every time Rania's friends mention one of their classmates, I just sort of nod as Rania explains to me who they are: Olivia Something, Ada on the Soccer Team, This Eighth-Grade Boy Named Colin Who's Incredibly Cute. It feels like she's translating for me, or adding subtitles to the conversation—and I have this prickly feeling that hanging out with Journey is easier than hanging out with my best friend.

Overnight, I can't sleep at all. At seven the next morning, I write a note that I leave on Rania's desk—*Thanks for inviting me!* ☺, *L*—and almost escape. But maybe she hears me pack up my sleeping bag, because just as I'm about to slip out of her house, she's at the front door.

"Lyla, you're leaving so early?" she's saying. "You sure you can't stay for breakfast? Mom's making waffles!" Rania's voice is a loud whisper, probably because everyone else in the house is asleep. Her breath smells stale, like she needs to brush her teeth.

"I just really have to get home now," I say. "Sorry."

"Oh. Well, I hope you had fun."

"Yeah, I guess." My mouth smiles.

"Call me later?"

"Maybe. I have a ton of homework. And my family has plans today, so."

I'm sure she can tell I'm lying. Because if your family actually does have plans, you say what they are. And I don't.

This time when Rania throws her arms around me, I don't stagger. "Well, thanks for coming, Ly."

"Bye," I say into her shoulder, and run out the door.

ONE-ON-ONE

When I get home about fifteen minutes later, Mom is in the kitchen drinking coffee. She's in her exercise clothes—a University of Maryland tee and yoga pants. Her hair looks sweaty, like she just got off the treadmill. Which reminds me of Journey's mom, and Journey's house, and Journey.

"Lyla!" she almost shouts. "You startled me! I didn't expect you home so early! Everything okay?"

"Sort of," I say as I sink into a chair at the table. "Rania had some other friends over from school. It was . . . not what I was expecting."

"Really? What were you expecting?"

"I don't know. Time alone with her, I guess. Because it feels like I never see her anymore."

Mom smiles sympathetically. "I hear you, sweetie. One-on-one time is so important, isn't it. Although don't you think it's good to branch out a little, make some new friends? I know you and Rania have been so close, but to be honest, I've always worried you girls were a little too dependent on each other. And now that you're almost teens, it's probably healthy for you both to expand your—"

"Yeah. I guess."

She sips her coffee. "And anyhow, *you're* making some new friends also, right? Like Journey."

I shrug. "I barely know Journey. And she's not a friend like Rania."

"I know, but give it time. And maybe you can become friends with Rania's new friends."

"Mom, that definitely won't happen. Those girls are all different from me."

"How are they different?"

"They're just . . . incredibly sporty. They gossip a lot. And they think writing is dumb."

"They *said* that?"

"No, not exactly. But when I told them about my story, that's how they acted."

"Well, not everyone's into fantasy books, right? And just because they're not into writing doesn't mean they think it's dumb. I wonder if it's possible you misread their reaction. If Rania's friends with these girls, why not give them a chance?"

"Yeah, maybe."

Why is Rania friends with them, anyway? They're all so different from her, too!

Except . . . what if that's not even true anymore?

What if I've lost track of who she is?

Mom gets up to pour herself more coffee. "Ly, have you had breakfast yet? I was about to toast some English muffins."

I realize I'm starving, probably because I didn't eat much dinner last night. "English muffins sound great," I say.

I watch Mom split the English muffins with a fork and pop them into the toaster oven. While they're toasting, Mom sits again, drinks more coffee, and looks at me with serious eyes. "Anyhow, I'm glad we have a minute to talk, just the two of us. I know Dad and I have been focused on your sister lately, and I wanted to say I feel terrible about all the fighting. I'm sure it hasn't been easy on you."

So she noticed. "Yeah. It hasn't, actually."

"I know, sweetie, and I'm sorry. It's just a very stressful time right now. We're trying to be supportive, but Dahlia is refusing our help."

"Maybe she doesn't want any help."

"Yes, but maybe she needs it."

"What if—"

Mom blinks. "What if what?"

"Nothing." My heart is pounding. I almost blew it, didn't I? "What if you just let her figure out what she wants to do? With her college essay, I mean."

Mom rocks her head from side to side like she's weighing pros and cons. "Trust me, Dad and I would love to do that! But the reality is the college process has strict deadlines, especially for kids applying early decision." She sips more coffee. "Anyway, I promise we'll get past this very soon. I *know* she'll produce a brilliant essay, the way she always does. Your sister is a very talented writer, just like you."

The toaster oven dings.

But my sister isn't like me, I tell myself. *Not even one tiny bit.*

FEEDBACK

In ELA on Monday it's like my brain is drowned in slime. Every time I think I might have an idea, I can't get it going. I just keep thinking about the sleepover—how I told Rania's friends I was writing a whole series. *And* entering the writing contest. So now they're expecting *The Lightning Thief* from me, and what if I can't even finish a first chapter? What if Orion wins all the prizes and I don't even get honorable mention? Those girls will turn me into the biggest joke at Dickinson. And probably Rania will laugh too, to fit in.

I yell at myself to just write anything, but every word feels like a boulder I'm pushing uphill. When I read what I've written, it's like all the boulders come crashing back down to flatten me.

I feel like crying. Or throwing my notebook into the trash.

Why did I tell anyone I could do this? What made me think I could write a whole book? Or even a short story?

What if I never write one good sentence for *the entire rest of my life*?

Aster's story will stay snarled in my brain forever, like hair clogging a sink. But of course I'll keep thinking about it, torturing myself with subplots and minor characters. Wondering why I couldn't fill up a notebook, like Stella.

Maybe it's because I'm not a writer after all.

Maybe I have zero talent. At anything! Even though I told everyone—including my family—that I did.

I rip out the page.

"Omigod." Stella turns around and glares at me. "Lyla, will you *please* try to be more quiet?"

"But I didn't say anything!" I protest.

"Yes, but you keep sighing and groaning and crumpling paper! It's incredibly distracting."

Now other kids are staring at us.

"Sorry," I say.

I decide to just work on the family tree. This is something I can do without groaning or crumpling, and at least it'll keep my pen moving.

I flip to the back of my spiral notebook, draw another branch, and start filling it in. For some reason, these names come easily: Juniper, the long-lost cousin who betrayed her family to join the Defectors. Lord Villacius, married to Lady Mallenthorpe. Whose secret identity is Oleander the Witch, head of the coven that haunts the Quagmire.

I do this family tree for a few minutes, and then it hits me: You know what I really need? A map! Because how can I write about all these different characters in all these different kingdoms, and the way Aster has to sneak across the Quagmire to rescue her sister, if I don't have a sense of the geography? And this landscape is super complicated, with woods and rivers and villages, so probably readers will need a map, too!

I start drawing. One time I look up and notice Ms. Bowman smiling at me, so I smile back. I can tell she thinks I'm writing, but I don't care. It's not like I'm cheating, right? Getting the map right is *extremely important*.

Suddenly Ms. Bowman is clapping her hands. "All right, can I have your attention, please, ducks and chickens?"

I put down my pen and look up.

"So I'd like us to try something today," she's saying. "We've been working on our stories for a week now, and at this point I think it's time for a little feedback."

"Feedback?" Harrison Greller says. "You mean from you?"

"I thought you weren't reading our stories until we were ready," Stella says. "Isn't that what you said?" Her eyes are huge, like she's scared she won't get an A-plus.

"No worries, Stella," Ms. Bowman replies. "I just mean it could be useful to share a page or two with a classmate. Writers often share unfinished work with readers. It keeps them on track."

"What if you're not sure you *want* anyone to read it?" Noah asks. He looks worried.

"Just choose any bit you feel comfortable sharing. One paragraph is fine, even one sentence. I promise, ducks and chickens, your work will benefit from sharing even the smallest passage with a reader."

By now I've turned into a frozen block of sweat. A paragraph? A sentence? I don't even have a single word that's worth sharing!

"All right, fine," Stella says. "I'll trade notebooks with Lyla."

What? No!

Before she can grab my notebook, I plop it on Noah's desk. Because he's in the same boat as me; neither of us has made any progress, so we'll be nice to each other, right?

His eyes bug at me.

"I haven't written very much," I mutter.

"Same," he mutters back. "Just don't read the last five pages; they aren't finished. You can read anything before that. But none of it's good, really."

Noah's written more than five pages?

Crap.

Maybe we're not in the same boat after all.

QUICK PEEK

I'm pretending to read Noah's story—a ton of description about robots and lasers, written in tiny, super-neat handwriting—as I peek at his reaction to my notebook. He glances at the first page, which is nothing but crossed-out scribbles. Then he flips to the back. But of course that's just the family tree, and the start of a map.

"What do I do with this?" he asks me in a normal voice.

"Shh!" I shoot lasers at him with my eyes. "It's called pre-writing, okay? My story is extremely complicated, so

I've just been planning it out first. The characters, the world they're in, everything."

"Yeah, but." He scratches his cheek. "There's like . . . nothing here for me to read, Lyla. Or give you feedback about."

Stella turns around to stare at us. "What's going on?"

"Nothing," I say over my thumping heart.

She leans across Noah's desk to see my map. "Lyla, this is all you've done so far? Just some *pictures*?"

"It's part of my story, okay?" I say through my teeth.

"And what's this list? Cheeseweed, Turtlehead, Cow Vetch . . . ?"

"Just a list of names I'm planning to use. Or not. It's really none of your business, Stella."

Instead of looking annoyed when I say this, Stella looks sorry. Or just sorry for *me*. "Hey, Lyla, I'm not trying to hurt your feelings," she says. "And I apologize for saying shut up before. I didn't know you were having so much trouble."

I swallow.

Her big dark eyes get bigger. "You want some help? I'm really good at writing."

Hearing this horrifies me. Help from Stella Ramirez, who isn't the slightest bit creative, who only cares about grades and trophies? I can't think of anything in the universe I want less.

"No thank you," I tell her. Too loudly, probably, because now Ms. Bowman is standing by our desks.

"Everything okay over here, friends?" she asks.

"Lyla hasn't written anything yet, so Noah has nothing to critique," Stella informs her.

Ms. Bowman blinks. "Ah," she says. "All right, Stella, back to your own reading now, please. Okay if I take a quick peek at your notebook, Lyla?"

I nod, because seriously, what choice do I have?

My teacher's eyes meet mine. "Is there a part I should avoid? I don't want to read anything that's private, or that you don't feel comfortable sharing."

"No, it's all fine." I feel nauseous as I hand her my notebook.

I barely breathe as she flips through the empty pages until she finds the family tree and the map and the list of weird flower names. She's nodding a little as she tucks some hair behind her ears.

Is it possible she *doesn't* think I'm messing up . . . ?

No, that can't be right. Because of course I am! It's completely obvious.

Finally she hands the notebook back to me. "Wow, Lyla, I see your creative wheels are really turning! Do you think we could chat a bit after class?"

"You mean today?" My voice is squeaking. "But after class is lunch. And we're having a math test right after that, so I'll need to eat."

"It'll only take a couple of minutes. I promise you'll have plenty of time for lunch."

I nod, because again I obviously have no choice.

"Sorry, Lyla," Noah mumbles as Ms. Bowman walks away.

"Not your fault," I tell him, sighing.

When the bell rings, I pretend to tie my sneaker until everyone is out of the room. Then I go over to Ms. Bowman, who's frowning as she's typing on her laptop. It's not an unhappy frown, more like she's concentrating extremely hard.

Is that how I look when I'm writing? Probably not. Probably I look ready to burst into tears.

She closes her laptop and smiles at me. "Ah, good, Lyla. So I thought we could talk about your story?"

"Sure." I swallow. "What about it?"

"Just about getting started. Perhaps I can help? Sometimes when a writer is stuck it helps to talk it out."

"I know," I say quickly. "But I'm not stuck." Because it's one thing to talk it out with Rania, or even Journey. It's a completely different thing to discuss my writing *with Ms. Bowman*.

I mean, of course I want to impress her with my story, once I get it down on paper. But also (and I didn't realize it before this minute) I want her to think of me *as a writer*—someone who turns out stories and characters like *eh, no sweat*. Someone who's *talented and creative*, not just the sort of student who does great on tests, like Stella or my sister. Someone who doesn't need a writing tutor or a helper or whatever Ms. Bowman is trying to be.

I don't even know why this matters to me so much, but it does.

My teacher is studying my face like it's a road map of Mars. "So can you tell me something about the plot?"

"Yes, but it's incredibly complicated. So I'd rather just write it, if that's okay. And I do think I'm ready now. To start."

I say this fast, without breathing, because all I want is to escape.

"All right, then," Ms. Bowman says quietly, after a few seconds. "But there's absolutely no pressure here, Lyla. No one expects you to produce a masterpiece, or even a finished story. My goal is really just that folks enjoy the writing process, with no rules or expectations."

"Okay."

"So if it helps, maybe try writing yourself a note to keep on your desk. Something like: *First drafts don't need to be per-*

fect; they just need to be written. Because you'll always have time to revise later, you know?"

I nod.

"Anyway, I hope you don't feel as if I'm forcing you, or even encouraging you, to enter that writing contest. Like I said, it's completely optional."

"I know, but I *want* to enter. I mean, I'm definitely entering!"

Ms. Bowman tucks some hair behind her ears. For the first time I notice all the holes on her earlobes. Maybe in her other life as a rock star she wears a bunch of earrings. I wonder if that looks cool on her, or weird.

"Well," she's saying. "You know that I'm here for you, Lyla. Feel free to bounce ideas off me, or help you brainstorm, or even just chat about your story. Anytime. If you ever *do* feel stuck."

"Thanks," I say. "But I'm sure I won't. Feel stuck, I mean."

The way she blinks, I can tell she doesn't believe me, but at least she doesn't argue.

I clear my throat. "Can I please go to lunch now? I'm starving, and next period—"

"Yes, you told me. Good luck on that math test, Lyla," she says as I run out the door.

WORD PERSON

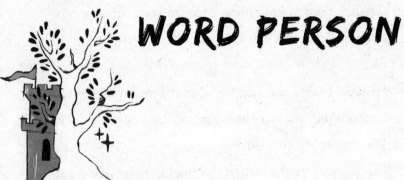

After that conversation I don't go to the lunchroom, where I know Journey is waiting for me. I'm not exactly sure why I don't; I had a surprisingly good time at her house on Saturday. But after that sleepover at Rania's, and that conversation with my mom, it feels like the world has decided Journey is my new best friend from now on, and a part of me sort of wants to squirm away. Because it's like yes, she's a very smart person, amazing with animals, and definitely nice—but I can't help thinking she's a teeny bit desperate. And the way her mom grabbed my hand as I was leaving? I don't know. It just seemed weird.

Plus, right now I'm freaking about my story—not just the fact that it's a disaster, but also the whole thing with Ms. Bowman, who probably thinks I'm the worst writer in the class. Also how I looked in front of Stella and Noah, and probably some other kids too. Journey wouldn't care about things like that because she doesn't care about other kids' opinions. And it's not like I can talk to her about my writing problems, because she doesn't understand about that stuff either.

What's funny is that even as I tell myself all this, I feel guilty for leaving her in the lunchroom. I know that if I don't eat with her, no one else will either. And the thought of Journey in her chocolate-brown newsboy cap, sitting all by herself, pretending to focus on her melted cheese, gives me a stomachache.

Even so, I head over to the school library and read *The City of Ember* until the bell rings for math.

When I get home after school, there's a strange guy sitting at our kitchen table, reading his phone. He's kind of young, and sort of handsome, I guess, in a nerdy, glasses, needs-a-haircut sort of way.

He puts down his phone as Spumoni rushes over to lick my knee. "Hi," the man says cheerfully. "I'm Daniel Chen, here to work with Dahlia on her college essay. Are you the little sister?"

The little sister.

"I'm Lyla," I answer. "Nice to meet you."

"Nice to meet you, too! Pretty soon you'll be needing my help also, I guess." He grins.

"Oh no, I'm only in seventh grade," I inform him. "And I'm totally fine with writing essays! But thanks anyway. Where's Dahlia?"

"She said she needed to use the restroom."

"You mean the bathroom?"

He laughs. "Yes, the bathroom. I see you're a word person too."

Even though he says "too," like he's comparing me to Dahlia, I take "word person" as a compliment.

I can't help smiling as I go upstairs.

Although right away I see the bathroom door is wide open. If Dahlia isn't in there, where is she?

I peek into her room. She's sitting cross-legged on her bed, staring at her phone.

I clear my throat so I don't startle her. "Hey," I say. "I thought you said you were getting rid of your phone."

"Well, I needed to text Nico about something." Her fingers keep moving. "What's up?"

"What's *up*? Well, there's this guy in our kitchen. Daniel Chen? He says he's here to help you with your college essay."

Finally she looks at me.

"*And* that you're in the restroom," I add.

"Well, obviously, I'm not in any 'restroom,' am I." My sister rolls her eyes.

"So then . . . you're going back downstairs?"

"Theoretically."

"Okay, but when, exactly? Because he's waiting."

"Lyla, how is this your business?"

"Well, you can't just leave him sitting downstairs!"

"No? Why can't I?"

Is she kidding? "Because for one thing, Mom and Dad are paying him to help you."

"Sooo . . . I'll just have to pay them back, I guess. When I can."

My left eye twitches a little. "Dahlia, what's going on?"

"With what?"

"You. This college thing." She doesn't answer, so I add, "If this guy is here to help you with your essay, that means you haven't told Mom and Dad yet, right?"

"About what?"

"Come on, you *know*. What you told me, about not going to college."

"Shh!" She says this even though our parents are both at work, so obviously they can't hear. "Anyhow, it's my problem, not yours."

"But Dahlia—"

"Lyla, I'm under enough pressure right now. The last thing I need is pressure from *you!*"

"I'm not pressuring, okay? I just think—"

Her face is scrunching. "No, Lyla, you *don't* think! And you have absolutely no idea how I *feel!*"

"That's not true."

"Oh, but it is! It's like you go to play school compared to me, basically just to hang out with your little friends! And where the teachers tell you how great you are *all day long*, and nobody expects anything, and every single grade, every decimal, doesn't count for your *entire future!*"

"What are you talking about, Dahlia? School is hard for me, too!"

"Yeah, *right.*" She hugs a pillow in front of her chest. "You know what, Lyla? I think you secretly *love* seeing me all stressed out like this. Because you're jealous."

"Excuse me?"

"You've always *been* jealous! All my grades, all the attention I get—it makes you feel bad about yourself, doesn't it? So you're giving me a hard time—you're standing in my bedroom *lecturing* me—because finally you can feel superior to me about something!"

I open my mouth to answer. But then I close it, stomp out of her bedroom, and slam the door to mine.

JEALOUS

My head is on fire. My eyes are stinging with hot tears. Jealous of Dahlia?

All right, so maybe I am, a little. Although how could I *not* be, really? She's smart and beautiful and popular. Everyone's favorite. Great at everything she ever does!

But why is she acting like such a spoiled, selfish baby? Hiding in her room, being rude to that essay guy downstairs, not telling Mom and Dad the truth about how she doesn't want to go to college. Why would I be jealous of someone who acted like *that*?

Besides, the two of us are *completely different people*. I have *zero* desire to be the superstar student and model citizen! I'd much rather be the creative one, the writer. Even if I haven't written a single sentence—

A knock on the door.

"Um, yeah?" I call out hoarsely.

"Rania's here," Dahlia announces.

"What?" I jump off my bed, open the door, and stare at my sister. "She *is*? Where is she?"

"In the kitchen. I went downstairs, and there she was, talking to Daniel Chen." Dahlia does a small sideways smile. "By the way, Ly, I decided you were right. It's not *his* fault that Mom is stressing me out so much. And since we're paying him all this money—"

But I can't even listen to this now. "Wait, why is Rania downstairs? Why didn't you tell her to come up?"

"Because you had a fight with her, didn't you? At that sleepover thing."

"We didn't fight! Who told you we did?"

"I dunno, Mom said something? Maybe I misunderstood. Anyway, should I send her up?"

"Yes! Of course you should!"

"You're *welcome*, Lyla."

As Dahlia heads back downstairs, I race over to the box

of tissues I keep on my desk, and blow my nose. I grab a second tissue for my eyes. Then, for some reason, I finger-comb my hair. Why should I care how I look to Rania? I've never cared about this before.

Fifteen seconds later Rania is in my room, wearing a tie-dye Dickinson sweatshirt and a camouflage-patterned backpack. She isn't smiling.

"Hey, Lyla," she says softly. "You never called me yesterday."

"I told you, my family had plans," I answer. "I was busy all day! Don't you have track practice now?"

"Mr. Verplanck canceled it. Dental emergency."

For a second I have this image in my head: the dental ambulance. Sirens, flashing lights, a voice on a megaphone: *Make way, folks, a cavity!* I almost tell this to Rania, but I can see she's not going to laugh.

"So . . . what's going on?" I ask.

Rania sits on the edge of my unmade bed. "I'm not sure, to be honest. I just have the feeling that maybe you're mad at me or something."

"I'm not mad, Rania."

"Well, the way you left my house yesterday—"

"I told you, I had to get home."

"Okay, whatever." She sighs. "So is it about my friends?"

I decide to give up. Because it's impossible to hide anything from Rania; she knows me too well. "Yeah," I admit. "They just made me feel . . . I don't know. Stupid."

"About what?"

"Everything. My writing, mostly."

"Lyla, you—" She stops herself. Her face is pinched.

"Me what?"

Rania twists her hands. "Look, I don't want to hurt your feelings, okay? But the way you were talking about your story, and the writing contest? You were kind of bragging, really, and you wouldn't stop. So of course they reacted."

My throat gets tight. "Rania, I only said all that because they made me feel weird about not doing track. And going to an old, depressing school!"

"Whitman isn't that old. Or depressing."

"That's what I told them! And not everyone has to be all sporty, right? It's okay to do other things besides track!"

"No one's arguing, Lyla."

"Well, *they* sure were! Especially Maeve." Now my eyes are stinging again, and my voice is wobbling. "Can I say something, Rania? When you invited me over, I thought it would be just the two of us."

"You did? Why?"

"Because—" Oh great, now my eyes are leaking.

"Because I miss you, okay? I feel like we never spend time together anymore, not like we used to. And I thought you missed me, too."

"I *do m*iss you, Lyla! Of course I do! But I've made some new friends, and I'm really happy about that, actually." She pauses. "Haven't *you* made any new friends at Whitman?"

"Well, one, I guess. This girl called Journey."

"Journey? That's a funny name."

"I think it's cool." I shrug. "I wouldn't say we're super close. But yeah, we're friends." When I hear myself say this, I remember how I left her alone in the lunchroom, and I feel a jab of guilt. "She invited me over on Saturday. That's where I was before the sleepover."

"Really? That's good to hear, because . . ." Now Rania is biting her lip. "Can I ask you something, Lyla? When we were in fifth grade, didn't you feel like we were in our own little world? And that you were missing out on other things? Other people? And weren't you a teeny bit bored with just *me* all the time?"

I'm too shocked to answer any of those questions. All I can do is shake my head.

"Well, that's how I felt," Rania says. Her voice cracks like shrinking ice. "How I *feel*. Lyla, I'm still your friend, okay? I just think we both need other friends too. And what I've been hoping is that you'll be friends with my Dickinson friends also. That's why I invited everyone for the sleepover."

Now I'm just flat-out crying. "But why *would* I be friends with those girls? They're totally different from me! In every way!"

"Well, but maybe if you get to know them—"

"What's the point, Rania? Because the only thing we have in common is *you*."

I grab another tissue to wipe my face. Rania twists the end of her ponytail and stares at my rug.

We stay like this for a minute. Which is an extremely long time when you're wondering what else to say.

Finally Rania gets up from my bed. "You know, Lyla, I'm trying very hard to stay friends with you, I really am. But if I can't include you, if you won't *let* me include you, it's like I'm trapped in the middle. Like you're basically forcing me to choose sides."

And that means I lose, right? I think as I watch my best friend leave my room.

DISAPPEARING

All right, this is it!

No more family trees or maps! Or wasting time over names! Or thinking about Dahlia and Rania! And all of Rania's new best friends. And how she's chosen them over me, basically.

This is writing time, the most important time of the day! A chance to block out everything, all my worries and problems, and focus on nothing but my story. And just try to tell it to myself, like I've been doing in my head.

Although as I stare at my empty page, I can't ignore the

fact that Ms. Bowman's eyes are on me. It's not too hard to guess that after yesterday she'll be checking my notebook. Even if she doesn't, it's time to start showing her what I can do. I mean, if I'm a writer the way I think I am, the way I keep telling people I am, I need to stop procrastinating and obsessing and distracting myself and just, finally, at last, *write*.

So here I go:

> *Aster and Verbena lived in the kingdom of Verplanck, on the edge of the Quagmire. They were sisters, but nothing alike—*

Ugh. Sounds like a fairy tale for babies. Delete that. Start over.

> ~~*Aster and Verbena were sisters, but completely opposite.*~~
>
> ~~*They were sisters, but no one could tell.*~~
>
> ~~*They were sisters, but totally different.*~~
>
> ~~*They were sisters, but—*~~
>
> ~~*They were sisters—*~~

"Lyla, you okay?" Stella is turning to look at me with pity eyes.

"Fine. Just trying to write this."

"Need a tissue?"

"What? No thanks."

"Well, let me know if you change your mind."

~~They were sisters, but~~

~~They were sisters~~

~~They~~

~~They~~

~~They~~

I run out of the room in tears.

For some reason I end up in the school library. The librarian, Ms. Rosen, is a youngish woman with freckles and short, curly brown hair. On her desk are a bunch of dog photos in clear plastic frames—she has three black Labs—and a small box of tissues.

I guess she notices that I desperately need to wipe my nose, because she hands me the whole box of tissues. "Can I help you with anything, Lyla?" she asks, smiling a little.

Does she remember I was here yesterday, too?

"I just need to look up something," I say. "For a project. In ELA."

Right away I think that's too much information. But Ms. Rosen is still smiling.

"Ah," she says. "You're in Ms. Bowman's class, right?"

I nod.

"She's such a great teacher, isn't she? Well, let me know if you need anything, okay? I'm not expecting any classes this period, so I'm available to help."

She starts poking through the returns bin. I grab a copy of *Princess Academy* and bring it to a seat in the corner, over by the atlases and war books.

Just tune everything out and read, I tell myself. *Pretend no one can see you.*

Which won't be hard to do, really. Because reading is kind of disappearing.

Writing is . . . the opposite. A kind of appearing.

And what if disappearing is what I do best?

WRITER'S
BLOCK

yla, aren't you hungry?" Journey is asking.

About twenty minutes later I'm in the lunchroom, sitting at my usual table, nibbling a flabby slice of pizza. When the bell rang at the end of the period, I considered staying in the library. But I decided against it, because it was bad enough that Ms. Rosen knew I was supposed to be in ELA. If she noticed I was in the library two lunches in a row, she might report me to a counselor or someone like that. Maybe she'd think I was hiding out from the lunchroom, scared of a bully. And then I'd have to explain: *Actu-*

ally, what I'm scared of is blank paper. A whole notebook full of nothing.

Plus, I don't want to leave Journey by herself again.

"Lyla?" Journey's voice is too loud. She blows on her hot, drippy taco. I'm sitting across the table, so some of her spicy breath lands on me too. "You seem a little out of it. You okay?"

"Not really," I answer. "It's that story I was telling you about. It's driving me nuts."

"Huh." She thinks for a second. "Well, maybe it's the wrong story, then."

"Excuse me?"

"I mean, if it's fighting against you so hard, why not write something else?" She shrugs. "Or just do something completely different."

I don't say anything. But I'm thinking: *See? Journey doesn't understand anything about writing! You don't just walk away from a story you're fighting with! You keep fighting back! Even when you think you're going to lose.*

But maybe . . . I don't know. What if she's sort of right, and there's a way to do something different? I mean with the same story. Although I can't imagine what that would even be.

"Oh, there you are, Lyla!"

It's Stella Ramirez, of all people.

Crap.

"Okay if I join you?" she asks, sitting before we can answer.

Journey's eyes meet mine. I can see she's not too happy about this. I wonder if they know each other from sixth grade, or possibly back in elementary.

Stella is ignoring Journey as she takes a bite of her tuna sandwich. "So where'd you go last period?" she's asking me.

"Just the library," I say.

"Oh, that's what I thought. You know, Ms. Bowman was really worried about you. She called the principal."

"She *did*?"

"Well, yeah! Of course she did! A kid runs out of her classroom crying hysterically—"

"You were crying?" Journey's eyes pop at me.

"But I wasn't *hysterical*," I say through my teeth.

"All right, but you were still crying," Stella argues. "I *saw* you, Lyla. Anyway, Ms. Bowman got a call like two minutes later, and I couldn't hear very much, but it sounded like she said the word *library*. So I figured that's where you went. Were you freaking out again about your writer's block?"

"I don't have writer's block," I mutter.

Although as I'm saying these words, I'm wondering why. I mean, why not just admit it, finally? Obviously I *do* have writer's block. Because what else would you call this terrible sort of frozen-ness, the fact that I can't write a sentence, or even just one word, without telling myself it's the Worst Thing Ever on Paper? And crying and sweating, and immediately crossing it out?

But even if I admit this to myself—*I have writer's block*—I can't stand the thought of admitting it to Stella Ramirez.

Stella wipes her mouth with a napkin. "Well, Lyla, I meant what I told you before. I'm volunteering to read if you want to show me anything. I've already finished one story for the writing contest."

"What writing contest?" Journey asks.

Finally Stella looks right at her. "The town library one," she informs Journey. "They do it every year. Lyla, you planning to enter something too?"

"Oh, definitely," I say, avoiding Stella's eyes.

She smiles. "I had a feeling you'd say that. Anyway, I have some free time before I start my next story. So if you want any help . . ."

Her next story?

"That's very nice of you, Stella," I say. "But Journey's already offered, so I think I'm good now."

I shoot eye lasers at Journey so she doesn't blurt out

something like *I offered to help? ME? But I don't know anything about writing! And I told you before, I don't even read fantasy!*

She gets it, though.

"Yeah, I have some free time too," Journey says casually as she takes an enormous bite of drippy taco.

FREE WRITING

That whole afternoon I'm worried that Ms. Bowman is going to call my parents, or maybe even me, to discuss my freak-out during ELA. But no one says anything about it during dinner, maybe because my parents are too busy grilling Dahlia about Mr. Chen.

"So how's it going with the college essays, baby?" Dad asks her.

"I don't know. Fine, I guess," Dahlia says.

"What does that mean?" Mom presses. "Have you made any progress after that session with Mr. Chen?"

Dahlia sighs. "I don't know, Mom."

"You don't *know*? Dahlia—"

My fork clatters to the floor. I jump up from the table to get a new one, but all the forks are in the dishwasher. So I take one out of the dishwasher and wash it slowly, carefully, with extra soap. Then I announce I can't dry it, because all the dish towels are in the hamper, so I go upstairs to get one from the linen closet.

Anything to escape this conversation.

At the beginning of ELA the next day, Ms. Bowman has an announcement.

"Okay, snickerdoodles," she says. "For the first few minutes of class today, before we break into reading groups, we're going to try something new. Who knows the term 'free writing'?"

Harrison raises his hand. "You mean writing you don't have to pay for? Like when you download a book from the internet?"

"That's called piracy, Harrison," Stella says. "And it's pretty much stealing, for your information."

"Yes, Stella, it is," Ms. Bowman says. "But it's not what I'm talking about, friends. Free writing is a kind of warm-up exercise, like what musicians do before they play." She crinkles her eyes. "I don't know how many of you know this, but I play bass in a band. And before a gig, or even before a rehearsal, we all warm up our fingers, get our instruments in tune. So I'm thinking we might try a version of that as writers."

"You play bass in a band?" Noah asks. "Acoustic or electric?"

You can tell he's trying to distract Ms. Bowman so we don't have to do this free-writing thing. But she's too smart to fall for it.

"Electric," she says. "Happy to chat about that *later*, Noah, okay? So here's how free writing works: You choose any blank page in your writing notebook and write for ten minutes straight without stopping. The trick is that the whole time, you have to keep your pen or pencil moving. No pauses, no staring into space, no rereading what you've written. No worries about handwriting, or spelling, or grammar or punctuation. And no worries about it being good or even making sense. The point is just to keep the words flowing, without self-editing or even thinking. Hear that, snickerdoodles? *No thinking.*"

"Yeah, okay," Stella says. "But if we write without thinking, no one will understand it."

"No one needs to! This writing is just for you, whatever pops into your head."

"But what if nothing pops into your head?" Noah asks.

"Then just write that: *Nothing is popping into my head. Nothing is popping into my head.*"

Harrison guffaws. "That sounds dumb. But easy."

Everly Pak raises her hand. "Ms. Bowman, I really don't think I can do this without a topic."

"Same for me," Stella says, frowning.

Ms. Bowman nods. "So here's what we'll do. Those of you who choose to do this exercise without any prompts can just go for it: ten minutes of writing whatever you want. But if you do need a prompt, how about something open-ended like: What would your protagonist love to happen? What would your protagonist hate to happen?"

"But we can't answer those questions without thinking," Stella argues.

"The point is not to think about your *writing*," Ms. Bowman says. "Just let your ideas flow, without editing yourself or worrying about anyone else's reaction."

Is she saying this directly at me? I'm pretty sure she is.

I feel my face getting hot, probably turning red. Which means people can see, if they're looking. Is Ms. Bowman looking? If she notices I'm blushing, she's pretending not to.

Now she smiles at the class. "All right, we good, snicker-doodles? Then get out those writing notebooks. Ten minutes, no stopping. And *go*."

TEN MINUTES

Ten minutes? That's nothing, I can write for way more than that! At least I used to be able to before this class, which is crazy because I love ELA, I love my teacher, and I love to write, so it's incredibly weird that I'm having writer's block or whatever you want to call it. Keep writing keep writing. Here I go, moving my pen across the page. Who cares what I'm writing, I'm just barfing words, this is basically just word vomit. Sorry for that image but we're not supposed to self-edit or erase so I can't take it

back lol. Keep writing keep writing. Anyway here is some punctuation!!! I love exclamation points a lot!!! Also question marks, also the question mark/ exclamation point combination?!?!? Is punctuation writing?!?! It really should be if you ask me!?!?! Here is even more punctuation: &%#@^$ But it's not a curse word so calm down everybody ☺ Keep writing keeeeppp wriiiiiting!!! Now I am filling up this page with absolutely nothing worth reading why are we even doing this it's such a waste of time and ink. Speaking of which this gel pen is drying up oh no I'm running out of blue ink this is scary what if my pen runs out before the ten min- utes are up and everything I write is invisible??? Does it even count if no one can actually read the words??? Barf barf barf more word vomit more punctuation even if I'm the only one who ever sees

"Time," Ms. Bowman says.

TECHNIQUES

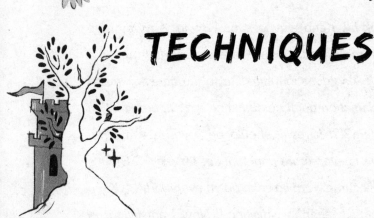

Hey, Lyla, can I steal you for a second?" Ms. Bowman asks.

We're in our reading groups after free writing. Our group is discussing *The Giver*, which is a book I have plenty of opinions about. So I don't want to leave the discussion, because I might miss something important. Although mostly I'm nervous about another chat with Ms. Bowman.

But obviously I have to follow her into the hall.

Is she going to scold me for running out of class yesterday? She hasn't said anything about it so far, but that doesn't mean she won't scold me now.

Or maybe she'll just be all sympathetic. Which in a way would be even worse.

"So what did you think about the free writing?" she asks.

I shrug. "Okay, I guess."

"I noticed your pen never stopped moving. Good work." She smiles. "I was just reading about this free-writing technique last night. Apparently many writers do it to get the creative juices flowing, you know?"

So it was for me, after all. Ugh, humiliating.

"Although there's no reason it wouldn't be helpful for other types of writing too. Like essays," she adds.

"I guess. But in sixth grade I never had trouble writing essays."

"Really? That's interesting, Lyla." Ms. Bowman's voice is like a pile of pillows. "So I wonder what's been different for you now. Is there something about *creative* writing that might be stressful? Perhaps because it's so open-ended?"

"No," I say quickly. "I really *love* that we can write whatever we want! Any *way* we want."

"Ah. So maybe . . . it's more about seventh grade?"

"Seventh grade?"

"I'm just wondering why you're so stressed, Lyla. And if maybe the writing thing isn't only about writing."

I swallow. "What do you mean?"

"Honestly, I'm not sure." Her voice stays pillowy. "I guess I'm asking if something else is going on. Like at home, maybe. Or with friends."

She's waiting for me to answer, but my mouth isn't working.

"Because sometimes when I'm stuck in my songwriting, I realize I'm actually stuck in something else. Like a relationship, for example," she adds.

I just shake my head.

"All right, Lyla. " She takes an extra couple of seconds as she looks into my eyes. "But I hope you know you can always talk to me. And not just about writing."

"Oh, I know. Thanks."

She tucks some hair behind her ears. "I also wanted to mention that I heard you went to the library yesterday, and I think relocating is another excellent strategy. So when we're writing in class, if you ever need a change of scene, feel free to head over there with your notebook. You don't need to ask permission, okay? Ms. Rosen says she's happy to have you anytime."

"Okay."

"I have a few other thoughts too. Can I share them?"

I nod.

"You ever do mindful breathing, Lyla?"

I shake my head again.

"So this is a very useful relaxation technique you might want to try. The way it works is you inhale to the count of four, hold your breath to the count of seven, and slowly exhale to the count of eight. It's great for de-stressing the nervous system, and you can even do it right there in your seat."

But already I'm imagining Stella: *Lyla, can you please stop breathing so loud? You're distracting me from my bazillionth story.*

"And if that doesn't do it for you," Ms. Bowman says, "another strategy would be going out into the hall and jogging in place for a minute or two. Or doing some jumping jacks, maybe. I'm a big believer in physical exercise to clear the mind. Do you have a dog?"

"A dog?" I blink at her. "Yeah, I do. His name is Spumoni."

"Well, if you get stuck when you're writing at home, try taking Spumoni outside for a walk! Exercise is always best in the fresh air! But at school, feel free to step into the hallway."

"Thanks," I say. "I mean, I can *try* all those things. But I don't see how they'll help my *writing*."

"These are just suggestions, Lyla. I know it's really hard to write—even to think straight—when you're feeling stressed." Ms. Bowman clasps her hands on her chest. "But keep talking to me, because I need to hear what's working for you and what isn't. We're learning together, okay?"

I know she's expecting something from me now—more thanks?—but all these techniques and strategies and thoughts are giving me a brain-ache. So I just ask if I can go back to my reading group.

"Sure thing," she says, almost like she's disappointed.

When I get home from school that afternoon, Daniel Chen is at the kitchen table with Dahlia, reading something on her laptop.

"Overall, it's much better, but can I be honest? It reads like something you think you're *supposed* to say, to impress your colleges."

"Yeah, but isn't that the whole point? To impress them?" she asks.

"Not necessarily. The best essays show who you really are. And college admissions people can always tell when an applicant's essay is from the heart."

The funny thing is that when he says this, Dahlia's face doesn't scrunch; she also doesn't yell, or run from the kitchen to hide in the restroom. She's actually listening to him, not acting like a tantrum-y baby.

As I grab some Chips Ahoy to bring upstairs to my room, I wonder if this is a good thing. Because okay—I'm relieved my sister isn't being rude anymore. But if she isn't going to college like she said, what's the point of wasting money on this college-essay guy? And why is she even working on her essay if she isn't applying?

Sometimes what people want from you is words. The more words the better. Just barf them on the page, no erasing or crossing out. No thinking, either.

So maybe Dahlia is writing to keep from thinking. And maybe writing is how she disappears.

NEXT DAY IN ELA

Yaaaayyy, more free writing!!! Those exclamation points are sarcastic, in case you were wondering. Okay so I have this story I've been thinking about it for a few months since like the end of sixth grade, keep writing keep writing. Anyway it's about these two sisters Aster and Verbena if that's her name I haven't decided probably I'll change it keep writing keep writing. My story is VERY complicated but the main plot is that Aster has to save her older sister who was always the favorite, and now she's chosen

to be Vanguard, which sounds like an honor, but Aster finds out it means her sister will be sacrificed in battle. The problem is to save her sister Aster has to cross the Quagmire which is an extremely dangerous dark swamp separating the kingdoms, full of Defectors (led by Aster's traitor cousin Juniper) who do this bloodcurdling shriek or shreik we're not supposed to care about the spelling. Also there's a mysterious one-toed Beast who keeps stalking Aster for some reason. Also there's a coven of witches led by Oleander (who used to be Lady Mallenthorpe, married to Lord Villacius) who makes Aster locate a magical gemstone before she'll let her pass. (Bleh, still need to think of a name for this gemstone!!!)

So I guess what Aster would love most of all is to cross the Quagmire to save her sister but also to be appreciated by their parents and everyone else who always pays more attention to Verbena who acts like she's perfect but isn't really, in fact she has a big secret she tells Aster. I haven't decided what that secret is, maybe she's in love with a poor scholar her parents disapprove of and they have plans to elope??? Keep writing, how much time is left??? I don't know, but already it feels like ten minutes and *my hand is tired!!! Ahhhggghhhh. And what Aster would hate most of all is failing, not just because Verbena is her sister even though sometimes they don't even get along. But also because every single person in the kingdom would know Aster tried to do something big and heroic but was too scared to actually accomplish*

"Time," Ms. Bowman says.

VOICES

Woohoo, another exciting installment of free writing!!! Three days in a row of this, so maybe ELA will just be free writing forever??? I'm keeping my pen moving like we're supposed to, but tbh I'm not sure what the point is keep writing. I mean when you write a book or a story or a college essay you need to choose every word super carefully. So seriously, what are we accomplishing with this technique or strategy or whatever we're supposed to call it? Here are some more words on this page. I

wonder if I'll ever do any of the stuff Ms. Bowman suggested if I feel stuck—breathe, jump, go to the library. The breathing and jumping seem pretty random, really. And if I go to the library I'll probably get distracted by all the books and just start reading to disappear. Although possibly the books will give me ideas??? That's what Ms. Bowman told me once. But the truth is I don't need ideas. Ideas are not the problem!! So what is? Keep writing keep writing. I don't know, but it's like I have too many people in my head—Ms. Bowman, Stella, Noah, Dahlia, my parents, all the judges in the writing contest, even Daniel Chen (which I know is sort of nuts). And I can't stop imagining all their opinions & feedback & criticism. Because if they don't think I'm a talented writer, then what AM I talented at???

And I guess mostly I'm thinking about Rania & her new friends, the way I kept bragging about my story & couldn't shut up. Bleh. I should have just told Rania about it in private, not that we ever get to be in private anymore. It's not like I think her friends are writing experts, but if I don't win the contest they'll think I'm a jerk. Which I guess they think now anyway. And maybe Rania will be embarrassed to *be friends with me? Though I have the feeling she already is.* 🙁

The other thing is that I know the story in my head is amazing but what if it's too complicated to get it on paper? Or just too complicated for ME. Also I keep thinking about all the books I love like The Lightning Thief and The City of Ember and The Girl Who Drank the Moon and compared to those, everything I write feels boring and babyish. And obviously I'm in seventh grade, so it's not like I'm competing with all those published authors!!! But my dream job is to be a writer one day, so it's EXTREMELY IMPORTANT to

"Time," says Ms. Bowman.

SIDES

A t lunch Journey is picking at her veggie wrap. At first I don't notice that she isn't eating, because I'm still thinking about ELA, especially the free writing I just did. I mean, I have to admit it felt good when Ms. Bowman gave me a thumbs-up, but of course the thumbs-up was just for moving my pen. And when you read a book, you never say to yourself, *Well, this book sucked, but look at all the typing that author did! Woohoo for word barf!*

After a minute, though, I can't ignore the fact that

Journey seems far away, not chatting or humming or eating with her usual messiness.

"Something wrong?" I say.

"I dunno." She blinks at me. "Lyla, can I ask you something? Do you know a girl named Gracie Rickwood?"

Do I? I put down my cheese sandwich. "Well, the only Gracie I know goes to Dickinson. She's tall and her hair is sort of red. And she's friends with this girl named Ayana."

"Yeah, that's her." Journey tears a corner of her napkin. She rips it into tiny bits, like confetti.

"Why are you asking?"

"Because she used to bully me. I saw her at my orthodontist yesterday, in the waiting room. I tried to ignore her, but she kept talking, pretending like she'd never been mean to me, you know? I probably should've gotten up from my chair and gone to the bathroom or something, but I didn't. I guess I wanted to believe she'd changed. But yeah, it was stupid." Journey's eyes meet mine. "Then she started saying all this stuff. About you, Lyla."

"About *me*? Like what?"

"It wasn't nice." Journey tugs on the brim of her cap like she's trying to hide her eyes. "Basically just how braggy you are, how you think you're so great. How you expect to win that big writing contest."

"I never said that, Journey!"

"But you told her about your story?"

"She's friends with my best friend—Rania, the girl whose sleepover I went to on Saturday? Gracie was there too, and so was Ayana. Also this other girl, Maeve. We were just talking about what we did. They all do track, so I mentioned my writing. That's the whole thing."

"Oh." Journey rips another corner off her napkin.

"You know those other girls too?" I ask. "Maeve and Ayana?"

"Uh-huh. Maeve was . . . *really horrible* to me in fifth grade. Like so bad my mom had to keep talking to the principal about it. But she wouldn't stop, and Gracie and Ayana joined in, so finally I homeschooled. Until Whitman." Her face pinches. "You're friends with them, Lyla?"

"I'm really *not*," I say. "And I'm sure if Rania knew all that stuff—I mean about the bullying—she wouldn't be either! Because Rania's my best friend; I know her very well!"

"Yeah, you said that." Journey sips some water.

"Okay, and I'll tell her about it, I promise. Rania will definitely want to hear this! But I don't understand why

Gracie even mentioned me to you. Or how she knows we're friends."

But as I'm saying this, I figure out the answer.

And my stomach knots, because this will mean another fight with Rania.

When I get home from school, Dahlia is sitting on the living room sofa with Spumoni and her friend-or-boyfriend Nico. *BeforeTimes VI* is on the TV screen with the volume up loud.

This shocks me, because Mom and Dad have a strict rule: No Boys if No Parents. So whatever Nico is, friend or more-than-friend, he shouldn't be here at our house when Mom and Dad are at work.

"Hey, Lyla," he says, grinning at me. Nico has wavy brown hair, a sharp jaw, and hazel eyes. He's definitely cute— although maybe that's not relevant if he's just Dahlia's friend.

"Hello," I say.

Dahlia flashes her eyes at me. "Nico and I are just taking a break from calculus. There's a big test coming up, so we're studying together."

"Uh-huh." I glance at the coffee table: no math textbooks or notebooks or calculators. Not even any pencils. Maybe

Dahlia sees me notice the empty table, because she turns to Nico. "One sec," she tells him, and pushes me into the kitchen.

"Lyla," she says. "You won't tell Mom, right?"

"About what?"

"Don't play dumb! That Nico's here, obviously. But I swear, it's fine, we were *just now* doing math—"

"You don't *look* like you were. And why do you need to study *with* anyone, anyway? You're amazing at math!"

"Yeah, well, not lately."

"What do you mean?"

"To be honest, I'm kind of failing calculus these days."

I stare at her. "You *are*? But you're this *total genius*—"

"Not this semester, okay? Actually, the only class I'm passing right now is Spanish, although I still need to turn in a big report about the Incan Empire. And it's two days late already." She winces. "Look, promise you won't tell Mom and Dad, okay?"

"Dahlia, they'll find out as soon as they see your report card! You can't hide it forever."

"Yes, Lyla, I realize that."

We stare at each other.

"And you know what else?" My voice is squeaking. "I'm really getting tired of all this."

"All this what?"

"The way you're making me keep your secrets."

My sister groans. "Omigod, Lyla. Is this *still* about the college thing? Why are you so obsessed with that?"

"I'm not obsessed! It's just that I live here too, remember? And lately it's all anyone ever talks about!"

"Well, I can't help it if Mom and Dad won't let it go! And you're *my sister*, so I really wish you were on my side for once!"

This feels like a kick in the stomach. "I *am* on your side, Dahlia! Of course I am! That's why I keep trying to help you!"

"Did it ever occur to you that I don't *need* any help? And maybe all I'm asking for is a little support?"

"Like what? What kind of support?"

"I don't know, just one person in this house who actually *listens*. Who cares about my feelings. Who doesn't make it about *them* all the time!"

All of a sudden she bursts into tears.

I've never seen Dahlia look like this before: her face all pink and liquidy, her shoulders shaking. Right now she's not the beautiful older sister, not the perfect student. Not even the tantrum-y baby hiding from Daniel Chen. She just looks like someone who needs a hug. So I give her one.

"Thanks," she says into my hair. "Thank you, Lyla."

We stay like that for a few seconds. Then she pulls away and wipes her face with a paper towel. "I guess I'd better go back to the living room, or Nico will think I ran away. How do I look?"

"Great," I tell her. "Like you always do."

"Liar," she says, rolling her eyes.

WOBBLY

After this conversation with Dahlia, the last thing I feel like doing is fighting with Rania—even though I spent the whole afternoon getting myself ready, planning what I'd say to her. But now, seeing my big sister all weak and weepy, begging me, or anyone else, to care about her feelings—I don't know, it's like the fight just drains out of me.

I mean, I still think Dahlia is wrong not to tell our parents about the college thing, and I wish she'd make Nico leave our house. And of course I'm worried about how she's messing up right now—failing math (and I guess other classes too), behaving like Not Dahlia. But also, I can't help wondering if maybe she's right—I haven't been such a good sister. Not enough on her side, like she said. Not listening, not letting her tell me things. Not going inside her world.

So now I'm feeling sort of wobbly. Have I been a bad friend to Rania, too? Not listening when she tried to share her feelings? Even when her feelings hurt mine back?

All I really want to do right now is snuggle Spumoni, who's snoring on my bed, and also to disappear into a book for the rest of the afternoon. I tell myself that Rania's at track practice now, so even if I text her she won't answer anyway. Besides, maybe Journey's wrong about what Gracie said at the orthodontist. Because sometimes she doesn't follow conversations too well, right? So isn't it possible she misunderstood . . . ?

But no, I really don't think she misunderstood Gracie. Also, you don't misunderstand bullying that's so bad you need to homeschool. No reason to doubt what Journey told me.

So, okay, I definitely need to talk to Rania about her friends. And I need to do it fast, before I chicken out. Because I promised Journey, who's my friend too, whatever Rania's friends think about her.

UNSTUCK

I sit on my bed and eat some Oreos I took from the kitchen. I let Spumoni lick the crumbs off my face. Then I take out my phone.

Hey, I text Rania. You there?

I spend the rest of that Friday—and then the entire weekend—on fire, waiting for an answer.

ELEVATOR

On Monday in ELA Ms. Bowman says she wants to try something different. Not free writing, she says, as she holds up a hat sort of like Journey's. Except this one is bigger, and black, not chocolate brown.

"Each of you will pull a strip of paper from this hat," she announces. "Whatever it says, that's what you'll write for the next ten minutes."

"Can we lift our pens?" Everly asks.

"Sure," Ms. Bowman says, "but try to use the free-writing approach as much as possible. No worries about spelling, grammar, even handwriting, okay? And no self-editing; if you find a little critic whispering in your ear, just brush 'em away." She flicks something invisible off her shoulder.

Then she starts walking up and down the messy rows, stopping at desks to let people reach into the hat. I watch Everly frown at her strip of paper, and Harrison sigh, and Stella bounce in her chair, like she can't wait to get started.

When Ms. Bowman gets to my desk, I avoid eye contact. I reach into the hat and run my fingers over the strips of paper. *Maybe there's one here that's meant for me,* I tell myself. *And I'll know when I find it.*

But I guess I'm taking too long.

"Don't overthink this, Lyla," Ms. Bowman murmurs. "Just pick."

I grab a strip from the bottom, one I'm pretty sure no one has touched, as if that matters.

It says:

Your main character walks into an elevator. There's one other person in the elevator staring at your main character. After a minute the person says, "Excuse me, but I think I know you." How does your main character respond?

"Okay, chipmunks," Ms. Bowman is saying to the class. "Ten minutes. Go."

I open to a random page in the middle of my spiral notebook.

All around me I hear pens scratching, pages turning, kids shifting in their seats. Next to me Noah sighs and Stella's pencil whooshes without stopping.

Immediately my heart starts racing and my hands drip.

So here we go again. It's like I've just stepped one foot into the Quagmire, and already I'm completely lost.

Why is this so hard for me and so mindless for everyone else?

I'm supposed to be a writer, aren't I? That's what I keep telling everyone. And if I can't even do this stupid writing prompt without freaking out . . .

I reach for my blue gel pen, but I'm so jittery that I knock it to the floor. It rolls under Noah's chair, so I have to reach between his sneakers to get it. Just as I'm about to grab it, he moves his leg, and my hand brushes his shin. I mean *the skin* of his shin, because he's wearing track shorts.

"Sorry," I mutter as he throws me a confused look.

I take my seat. Ugh. It's bad enough that I accidentally touched Noah's naked leg, but also dropping my pen made me lose a few seconds of writing time. So now I'm definitely behind, and I haven't even started yet.

All right, what if I just write something like: *Aster*

ignores Other Person or gets out at the next floor. Because seriously, Other Person could be a weirdo. Also, her world doesn't have elevators.

Not ten minutes' worth of writing and definitely dumb, but better than nothing, I guess. Although why does Ms. Bowman only give us ten minutes, anyway? How can you possibly be creative with that kind of time pressure? I bet Rick Riordan doesn't keep a stopwatch by his computer. If he even writes on a computer. Maybe he has a spiral notebook like this one. I wonder if he uses gel pens—

A hand presses my shoulder.

"Lyla," Ms. Bowman says in my ear. "Let's step outside for a sec, okay?"

I follow her to the hall with a sick feeling in my stomach, because obviously she noticed my not-moving pen.

Is she going to make me do jumping jacks now? The floor is slippery out here, and my shoes have worn-down soles. And what if someone walks by and asks what I'm doing? What would I say? *"My brain is stuck, so I'm trying to shake it loose"?*

Ms. Bowman's eyes are on my face. "Remember what I told you, Lyla," she says quietly. "We just want to find what works for you. Do you have any suggestions?"

I shake my head.

"How about relocating to the library?"

"I don't know, maybe. But we only have ten minutes! By the time I get over there—"

"Forget about the clock, Lyla. Take as much time as you need. As you *want*, okay? How do you feel?"

"Me?"

"Yes, you. Right now."

"I don't know. Scared."

"Scared?"

"Yeah, scared I'll never write anything good. Like, *ever again*."

"Anything else?"

She wants more? "Also mad at myself, I guess. Frustrated. Jealous."

"Jealous? Of who?"

"People like Stella. Who just fill up their notebooks with anything. Even if it's terrible!"

If Ms. Bowman agrees, she doesn't show it. "So why not use all that?" she asks. "Write your feelings."

Write my feelings?

But my story is about Aster and her sister Whoever. Not about random people in elevators, and also not about my personal feelings! Because I'm writing a fantasy novel, not an autobiography!

UNSTUCK

Although one thing I know for sure: I can't return to my desk and just sit there with my not-moving pen, lost in the Quagmire for the next seven (or possibly six) minutes, listening to Stella's whooshing pencil.

So I go back inside the classroom, grab my notebook, and head to the library.

NOODLE PEN

You don't know me, Elevator Guy, even if you think you do. I have a lot I keep inside, a lot I don't show, or share with anyone in the world. It's not like I have secrets, although I try to keep secrets for people I care about, for example my big sister Hyacinth/Verbena. But mainly it's that I'm wondering what it means to be a Scribe. Thinking I'm not as good as a Vanguard, even if I'm not exactly sure what a Vanguard is. Feeling I have no power, like if I had to cross the Quagmire right this minute, I'd have no

defense against the Beast and the Defectors. Also jealous of everyone—especially other Scribes—who just do their jobs every day without wondering if anyone even notices.

And why do I care about getting noticed anyway? What's so great about getting noticed?? To be honest, I'm glad I'll never be a Vanguard like my sister. I actually like being quiet and private, at least most of the time. I also think it's good to be underestimated sometimes—like how I tricked Oleander the Witch into letting me pass through the Quagmire. (She made me find her some magic Cloudstone, but I fooled her with a nugget of Milktooth—a gem the Seer once told me about, which basically reverses all evil spells!!!)

So what I'm saying is that I wish people wouldn't assume I don't have feelings. Or talent. Or that they know me when they really don't.

For example you, Elevator Guy!!!

The words gush out of me.

I was in such a hurry to leave the classroom that I left my pen behind, so when I got to the library, I had to ask Ms. Rosen to borrow one of hers. It's not a gel pen—it says

MANNY'S HOUSE OF NOODLES on the side, and the ink is black—but for some reason I'm writing so fast it's like this noodle pen can barely keep up. I don't care about the clock, or how long I've been writing; all I know is that it's way past ten minutes, and no one is telling me to leave, so I don't.

And after the bell rings, it takes me a few seconds to register that Ms. Bowman is over by the graphic novels, chatting with Ms. Rosen. As soon as she spots me spotting her, she pulls up a chair at my table.

"So?" she says in a library voice.

"I've been writing," I admit.

"Ah." Ms. Bowman's eyes light up.

"But it's just this prompt," I say. "I mean, it's not my *story*."

"But maybe you can build on it, right? Anyway, it's great you were productive! Do you know what worked for you?"

"I'm not sure. Being in the library, I guess. Using this." I hold up the Manny's House of Noodles pen.

She smiles. "A different pen is always a good move. I'm a big believer in switching things up."

"Also not seeing Stella," I add.

Ms. Bowman doesn't say anything.

I decide to keep going. "And not worrying about the

ten-minute thing. I *hate* time pressure, especially for creative writing!"

"Yes, I can see that. Some people like deadlines; some people don't."

"And maybe . . ."

"Yes?"

"I don't know. Doing what you said. Writing my feelings."

"Interesting," Ms. Bowman says slowly, making the word four separate syllables. "And may I ask you a question, Lyla? When you wrote your feelings, did you do it in the first person? From the point of view of your main character?"

"Well, my story has two main characters, actually."

"But for this prompt you chose one?"

"Yeah. Aster, the younger sister."

"Hmm," she says. "So I wonder if that's a way forward—connecting your feelings with Aster's, and writing from her perspective. Instead of writing in the third person, about two different characters, or trying to describe their whole big, complicated world. It could be that keeping it personal and emotional frees you up a bit. Just a thought."

I don't argue. But I don't agree with her either. I mean, she could be right, but I need to think about this.

"And speaking of moving forward," Ms. Bowman says after a few seconds. "I wanted to mention what I just told the class—that we'll be wrapping up this creative-writing unit at the end of this week."

My mouth drops open. "Wait, we *are*?"

I suddenly remember how Ms. Bowman said we'd be doing creative writing "for a few weeks." Have a few weeks gone by already? It's weird how I've lost track.

She nods. "Yes. I wish we could continue all semester, but we do have a curriculum. And persuasive writing is next on the agenda."

I can't help it; I make a barf face.

She laughs. "You don't approve?"

"We did that last year in sixth grade. Mr. Delgado made us write five-paragraph essays. *Exactly* five paragraphs, not four or six."

"Well, no worries there, Lyla; I'm totally fine with four or six."

"Okay, but my story." I swallow. "I mean, I haven't even gotten started yet, not really. Today's just a prompt, so it doesn't count. And there's that writing contest. . . ."

"Yes. About that." She tucks her hair behind her ears. "I've been giving this some thought, and I have to tell you I'm actually sorry I advertised it to the class. I think it may have put too much pressure on certain people."

Certain people means me, I guess. I don't say anything.

"Lyla, I'm wondering if it makes sense to focus on your story rather than on the contest. Then you could write when you feel like it, just for fun. And you'll be able to do a first draft without thinking it has to be perfect."

"Yes, but I *want* to enter." My voice croaks. "It's extremely important to me!"

She cocks her head. "It is? Why?"

"Because—" But I can't finish.

I know I could just tell her the truth: *Because I bragged to Rania and her new friends.*

Because I want to do one thing—anything—better than Dahlia.

Because I've never won a trophy for anything. And if I can't win one for writing, I'll probably never win one. Ever.

Although something tells me she'd think those reasons aren't too convincing. (I mean, really, what's the *actual point* of a trophy? All it does is take up space on your shelf. Space that could be used for other things, like books.)

And if I told Ms. Bowman I wanted to impress *her*, she'd probably say something like: *Oh, Lyla, I'm here to teach, not to be impressed. And anyway, I'm already impressed by all your hard work, blahblahblah.*

"Because I want people to read my writing," I say.

"Fair enough, but contest judges aren't the only readers out there! I'd love to see your story when it's ready, if you'd ever like to share it with me. And I'm sure some of your classmates would love to read it as well. Noah, for example."

Noah? Where did she get *that* from?

Ms. Bowman leans toward me. "Lyla, you just said you don't like writing under time pressure. But you realize the contest's submission deadline is in two weeks?"

Two weeks?

"Oh, right." My voice is almost a whisper. "I forgot."

"Do you think that deadline will be tricky for you?" she asks gently.

I chew my lower lip. Of course that deadline will be tricky. How could it not be?

"You know," Ms. Bowman says, "if I could give you any advice, it would be to step away from your story and clear your head a bit."

"You mean gestate?"

"Exactly. That's what I do when I've hit a roadblock with my songwriting. Sometimes I share it with my partner, and we talk it out. That often helps. But sometimes I'd rather just exercise or meditate or listen to other people's music. Or take my dog, Barnabus, for a good, long walk." Ms. Bowman grins. "And if none of *that* does the trick, I watch YouTube and eat cookies. Which totally works too, by the way."

I bet she's expecting me to grin back, but I don't. "Stepping away" is kind of what Journey said when she told me to write something else if my story was "fighting me." That felt like she was saying to give up—and it kind of sounds like what Ms. Bowman is saying now.

My eyes fill with hot tears.

I think Ms. Bowman notices, because right away she adds, "But if you're serious about submitting to the contest, then absolutely go for it, Lyla. All I meant is that it's up to you. Your story, your choice. No pressure from anyone, especially me. And I'll be rooting for you either way."

REAL WRITER

I stay in the library during lunch, because I can't face Journey. I promised her I'd talk to Rania about her friends; if I go to the lunchroom, I'll have to tell her that Rania never even texted back. And since I told Journey that Rania is my best friend—I mean, since I guess it's still *technically* the truth—admitting that Rania ignored me all weekend would make me look like a total idiot.

For a minute I consider lying to Journey, telling her that I explained the whole thing to Rania, who swore she'd never have anything to do with those girls ever again—but

I can't bring myself to do that either. There's just something about Journey that makes lying to her feel extra wrong. Luckily, Ms. Rosen keeps granola bars in her office; she invites me to take as many as I want, and that's my lunch for the day.

At dismissal I consider rushing home to start on my book (or story, or whatever it is at this point). But I tell myself that if I'm going to write under deadline pressure, I need a clear head—and I won't be able to think straight until I talk to Rania.

If this was sixth grade, I'd probably just walk over to her house—but I know she doesn't go straight home after school these days. So I decide to head to Dickinson and catch her at the end of track practice. The tricky part will be getting her alone, away from Gracie, Ayana, and Maeve, but if she isn't answering my texts, I really have no choice, do I.

Today the weather is cold and windy, but at least I have on Dahlia's old sweatshirt. Did she ever wear it as much as I do? Maybe not—I don't remember.

I've walked about three blocks when I hear someone calling my name.

I turn; it's Noah. Although possibly I heard it wrong? Because why would he be calling *me*?

I slow down for him to catch up. Just in case.

"Hey," he says as he reaches my side. He's out of breath and also freezing, I bet, since all he's wearing is an *Animal Crossing* tee and track shorts.

My stomach flips as I remember what happened in ELA, how I touched his bare leg by mistake. Also what Ms. Bowman said—how Noah "for example" would want to read my story. Whatever that means.

"Where are you going?" he asks.

I tell him I'm meeting a friend at Dickinson.

"So am I," he says. "You know Orion Skinner?"

"Yeah, we were in elementary together."

"Actually, I knew that."

The wind tosses some hair in my face. Also in my mouth, so I have to fish it out, which is definitely awkward. "Then why did you just ask if I knew him?"

"Oh, because you can go to school with someone and think, *That kid's a brain, that kid's a jock*, whatever—but it doesn't mean you *know* them."

I have no idea what to say to that, so I keep quiet. Besides, we're crossing a semi-busy street, so I'm watching the traffic.

"Can I ask you a question?" Noah says as we get to the curb.

"Uh, sure."

"What happened today in ELA?"

Oh no. "You mean with your leg?"

"What?"

"I'm sorry. It was an accident; I was just reaching for my pen, and—"

"Oh, not that! I meant when you left the room and didn't come back. This wasn't the first time you left. Are you . . . okay?"

"Sort of. Basically." I keep my head down as I step over a crack in the sidewalk. "But I needed a break, so I went to the library. Ms. Bowman says I can go there whenever I want."

"That's nice. She's nice."

"She really is." Should I keep talking? He does seem interested. "She's trying to help. I've been having writer's block really bad."

"Yeah, I know. I saw your notebook, Lyla."

"Right, you did." I grit my teeth. "So Ms. Bowman's suggesting all these techniques to unblock me, like switching locations. Also some other stuff, like jumping jacks and breathing."

"Breathing?"

"Not regular breathing, slow breathing. To de-stress. She also said I should watch YouTube and eat cookies."

"Seriously?"

I nod.

"Maybe I should try that, too." Noah grins at me. "Although I'd rather eat chips. With guac and salsa."

"Yeah, well. She's just trying to clear my head. I think the free writing was supposed to do that too."

"And did it?"

"I'm not sure. Maybe a little?" I peek at him. "Did *you* think it helped?"

"Not so much. But I'm not a real writer like you."

"What?" I almost laugh. "Noah, how can you say that? I haven't written a single word, and you have all those pages—"

"Right, but they suck." He shrugs. "Anyhow, I saw those charts and maps in the back of your notebook, remember? It's like you're building this whole world; I bet your story's going to be amazing! Orion's, too, although his is like the opposite of yours. It's science fiction, about this killer droid."

"You read it?"

"Just some of it, but yeah. You guys are both incredible writers. Way better than me."

Suddenly I feel embarrassed, but in a good way. *Noah thinks my story will be amazing! Once it's actually a story, of course.*

UNSTUCK

I can't help smiling as we cross the road to Dickinson.

"Anyhow," Noah is saying, "when you write it—I mean, after you finish—you can show it to me, if you want. I'm a terrible writer, but I read a lot, so."

"You do?" I blurt. "I thought . . . I mean, I think of you as a math person."

"So you don't really *know* me."

Is he blushing? His face could be red from the freezing wind. Although, no, I think maybe I insulted him. *Crap.*

"And by the way, math people read," he adds.

"Sorry," I say quickly. "And thanks, Noah! Well, there's the track. I'm meeting my friend now—"

"Yeah, okay, bye," he says as if suddenly he wants to escape.

TROUBLE

Maeve is the one who sees me first.

The whole track team—Rania, Maeve, Ayana, Gracie, plus about eight other kids—is standing next to a man with a whistle around his neck. He's telling them something about a baton; when he says "yap," Gracie covers her mouth like she can't stop giggling. Like the way he talks never stops being hilarious to her, for some reason.

Then Maeve says something in her ear and points at me. "Incoming," she says loudly.

Rania's eyes meet mine. She waves her hand, not her arm, and she isn't smiling.

My mouth goes dry.

Mr. Verplanck says a few other sentences I can't hear. The team runs around the track three times, stretches for a few minutes, and then practice is over, apparently.

Rania says something to Ayana and walks over to me. Still not smiling.

"Hi," she says.

"Hi." The wind is tossing hair in my face, so I try tucking it behind my ears like Ms. Bowman. "Can I please talk to you a minute?"

"Sure. Go ahead."

"I mean in private?"

Rania's face tightens. "Right now? I need to change first, Lyla."

"That's okay, I'll wait."

She nods once and heads into the building.

Maeve, Gracie, and Ayana walk over to me.

I re-tuck my hair. Maybe the problem is I have too-small ears.

"Hey, Lyla," Gracie says loudly. "How's the writing going?"

"Fine," I say.

"Win any trophies yet?" Maeve asks.

Gracie giggles.

I swallow. "Win any track competitions?"

"Meets," Maeve says. "That's what we call them, Lyla, not *competitions.* And yes, actually."

We narrow our eyes at each other.

"Where's Rania?" Ayana asks.

"She went inside," I say.

"By herself?" Ayana frowns like it's weird that Rania can go somewhere without their permission. "Is she okay? Did she say anything?"

"She said she'll be out in a second. We're *meeting,*" I add, but Maeve has already turned her back on me. Anyway, it was kind of a dumb thing to say.

Rania's three friends go inside. They walk with their heads together, like they're telling each other secrets.

Off in the distance I spot Noah leaving with Orion. I think about what Noah told me—how Orion is writing a great story, how he's letting Noah read it. *Lucky Orion to trust a friend like that. I wonder what his story is about. I could ask Noah, I guess—but if he tells me, I'll probably feel like my story is competing. Which of course it will be. Once I write it.*

I take out my phone and check my texts, mainly for something to do until Rania gets back here.

Shockingly there's one from Dahlia two minutes ago:

Hey L, what time is Mom home today?

I type: IDK, the usual, I guess. Why?

Dahlia: I think maybe I'm in trouble??

Me: What happened? Is this about school?

Dahlia: When are you getting home?

Me: Soon. I'm at Dickinson. I need to talk to Rania about something.

Dahlia: KK. Nvm then.

Me: you want me to come home now? Because I will.

Me: Dahlia?

Me: You there?

I wait a few minutes, but she doesn't answer.

And finally Rania is walking toward me. She's still in track shorts, but now she's wearing an emerald-green hoodie that says DICKINSON in yellow letters.

So I guess green and yellow are her school colors? How come I don't know Whitman's colors?

"You want to go somewhere, Lyla?" she's asking. She doesn't seem too enthusiastic.

I'm still a bit shaky from my sister's text, because she hardly ever texts me. And I can't help wondering what she means by "in trouble." And why she's wondering about Mom. And why she didn't answer.

So it's like: I want to be a good sister, but I have no idea what I'm supposed to do. What Dahlia even wants me to do.

And the thing is, right now I really need to talk to Rania.

"Can we go somewhere quick?" I ask. "Because I need to get home soon."

Rania blinks. "Family plans?"

"What?"

"That's what you said when you ran out of my sleepover, right? You had *family plans*. And then I didn't hear from you."

"Rania, I told you I was sorry—"

"Whatever, Lyla." She points to the softball field. "Why don't we go sit on that bench behind home plate?"

We walk over to the bench without talking.

As soon as we sit, Rania turns to me. Her mouth is turned down at the corners. "Okay, so what's up?"

"I just wanted to talk. About . . . well, your friends, actually."

"My friends? You mean . . . ?"

"Maeve, Gracie, and Ayana. But first, can I ask you

something, Rania? Why did you tell them I'm friends with Journey?"

"Who?"

"Remember when we talked in my bedroom, and you asked if I made any friends at Whitman? And I told you yes, a girl named Journey?"

"All right, sure. What about it?"

"You told Gracie? How come?"

She sighs. "I forget the details. We were having a conversation about something, and it just came up."

"A conversation? About me?"

"Lyla, we talk about a lot of things."

"But why would you talk to them about *me*?"

"Why? Because they're my *friends*." Suddenly Rania's eyes get watery, although possibly that's from the wind. "Lyla, look—I don't want to hurt your feelings; I still care about you, okay? But I really don't know what I'm supposed to do. You won't let me include you with my friends. And you're so jealous lately, like you just want me all to yourself!"

The word "jealous" makes me flinch.

Rania keeps going. "It's like you want to turn back the clock to elementary—"

"That's not true, Rania!" I croak. "And speaking of elementary. Did you know your friends bullied Journey in fifth grade? Did they ever mention *that*?"

The wind snatches Rania's ponytail and tosses it over her shoulder. "You want to hear the truth, Lyla? What they told me is that Journey's weird. Obsessed with animals, for one thing."

"That's not weird; it's cool!"

"And that she chopped off all her hair."

Now I'm getting angry. "Yeah, to donate it. To *cancer patients*. Don't you think that's incredibly generous?"

"They said she always wore some ridiculous hat. Also that she had zero friends."

"Well, maybe that's because they picked on her! You know how it is—when a kid is bullied, other kids keep away."

"So you're saying it's *their* fault she had no friends?"

"I don't know. Probably yes."

"Oh, come on, Ly! Don't you think that's a little—"

"Journey told me her mom kept going to the principal, but even *he* couldn't stop them! So finally she gave up and just homeschooled. Until Whitman."

Rania pulls up her hood. "Lyla, I'm not going to argue about this, okay? Whatever happened to Journey in fifth grade was a million years ago, and neither of us was there, so we can't actually *know* how it was. Anyway, people change. We're *supposed* to change by middle school, aren't we? I know I have, so I bet my friends have too. Have *you*?"

The question stings like a slap.

Have I changed since I started middle school? I don't think so.

Although, yeah, I'm a lot less sure than I used to be. About a lot of things—including you, Rania. Because you never used to be so mean. Unless you were mean all along, and I just never saw it before.

And maybe this is what Ms. Bowman meant that time she was asking about seventh grade. Because what if she's right, and I'm stuck, but not only with my writing?

What if I'm stuck about Rania, too?

Rania sighs. "Can I ask a question, Lyla? Does Journey have any other friends now? I mean, besides you?"

I chew my chapped lips. "I really don't know."

"So what if the problem is Journey? Did you ever consider *that*?" Rania stands. "Sorry, I have to go."

"Already?"

"Lyla, you're busy and so am I. Family plans," she adds, and leaves me on the bench by myself.

COMMUNICATE

As soon as I open our front door, Spumoni jumps up at me, like he's frantic to pee. I take him out to our front yard for a couple of minutes, then go back inside to find Dahlia.

But she's not in the kitchen or the living room. Her bedroom is empty too. So is the bathroom.

So probably that means she was texting me from somewhere else. Like where? School, I bet. Maybe she stayed late to talk to her calculus teacher.

I take out my phone to look for a clue. Did she ever *say*

she was texting from our house? No—I just assumed that, because she asked what time Mom was getting home today.

I tell myself that I'll talk to her when she gets home. Anyway, after what happened with Rania just before, I have other things to worry about. Like the fact that I've lost my best friend, apparently. Who maybe I never knew as well as I thought I did.

I open my laptop.

> *Juniper? Is that you?*
>
> *Yes and no, Aster.*
>
> *What does that mean? You're still my cousin, aren't you?*
>
> *Only technically. I used to be your cousin Juniper. Now I'm Defector Number Thirty-Three.*
>
> *But wait! You're more than just a number! Don't you remember how we used to play together when we were little? And how we shared jokes—*
>
> *Defectors have no memory of their past lives, Aster. And you'd be wise to run away from me.*
>
> *But surely you can escape the Quagmire! Let me help you out of this awful place!*
>
> *Don't even suggest such a thing. The Quagmire is my true home now. SHREEEEEEK.*

❈ ❈ ❈

Mom comes home at five fifteen. Dad walks in the door twenty minutes later. I hear them in their bedroom, talking. The only word I can make out is "Dahlia."

Here we go, I tell myself. *Why is everything in this house always "Dahlia, Dahlia, Dahlia"?*

But the feeling lasts only a nanosecond. Because what did Dahlia mean by "trouble"? And where exactly is she? What if Mom and Dad don't know either?

A couple of minutes later there's a knock on my bedroom door.

Mom is in her after-work sweats and tee. She's taken out her contacts and is wearing the big red eyeglasses she wears only at home.

"Hey there, Ly," she says. "How was your school day?"

I shrug. "The regular. Another math quiz."

"How was it?"

"Okay, I think. I did the extra credit."

"That's good." She pauses. "Do you know where your sister is?"

I shake my head.

"She's not answering her phone," Mom says. "I've been calling and texting."

Now Dad is at my door too. "You hear from her today?"

I shake my head. Like it's not a lie if you don't use words.

He scratches his cheek. "Any theories why she wouldn't communicate?"

My heart is banging so loudly I'm sure they can hear it.

I want to be on Dahlia's side. I want to support her, listen to her, care about her feelings. And if I tattle on her—that she's in trouble, failing classes—she'll never speak to me again, I'm sure of it.

"Don't worry, she'll be home soon," I say. "She never misses supper."

"True," Mom says. "Okay, Ly, please go set the table. I'm nuking last night's chicken casserole."

I shut my laptop and go downstairs.

Fifteen minutes later, Mom, Dad, and I are eating. No one is saying much. It's like Dahlia is taking over the conversation the way she always does, except this time it's by not being here.

Finally Mom puts down her fork and wipes her mouth with a napkin. "Maybe I should call Sophie."

"Yeah, maybe," Dad says. "But do you really think she'd just go to a friend's house and lose track of the time?"

"What are you suggesting, Matt?" Mom asks.

"I'm not suggesting anything! I just mean it doesn't sound like Dahlia."

Okay, but haven't you noticed that lately she's Not Dahlia?

Mom gets up from the table and takes her phone out of her bag. She dials somebody, possibly Sophie's mom. I hear Mom's voice from the living room: "Yes, we're wondering too. Well, I'm sure you're right. But will you let us know if you hear anything? I will, absolutely, I promise. You too. Thanks so much, bye-bye."

Mom returns to the table. Her face is pale. "Dahlia's not at Sophie's, and Sophie says she doesn't know where she is. Okay, so now I'm definitely worried."

"I'm sure she's fine, Megan," Dad says.

"You are? Why?"

"Because Dahlia's got a good head on her shoulders. She doesn't do stupid things."

"Really? Have you been around her these past few weeks?" Mom's mouth twists.

Wait—did Mom just say that Dahlia was acting *stupid*?

"And by the way," Mom adds, "she's on track to miss the early-decision deadlines."

"What if she did?" I blurt.

My parents look at me.

"I mean, would it be so bad? Maybe Dahlia *wants* to miss the deadline."

"Lyla," Mom says, her eyes burning into mine. "Is there something we should know?"

My heart is banging. "Because like, what if she didn't go to college? It wouldn't be the worst thing in the world, right?"

Mom actually gasps. "I'm sorry, *what*?"

"Maybe she's too stressed out to go. And that's also why—" I force myself to stop. Too bad I can't do that four-seven-eight kind of breathing now, because I really need to de-stress.

"Also why *what*?" Dad is leaning forward, like he wants to jump at me from across the table. "Answer us straight, Lyla: Do you know where your sister is, or not?"

"I really don't, I swear." I'm barely breathing at all. "But she did text me a few hours ago."

"She did? Why didn't you tell us that before?"

I don't answer, because I have no idea what words to use.

It's hard to keep my eyes on my parents' faces. They both look frozen, panicked.

And now my head is exploding. Am I being fair to my parents if I stay quiet? Am I being fair to Dahlia if I don't? Because if she's "in trouble," how can I help if I don't even *try* to rescue her?

And how can I rescue her on my own, anyway? What if I just told my parents the truth?

Don't edit yourself. Just get the words out without thinking.

"Dahlia has a lot on her mind right now," I say. "She's super stressed about the college thing. I think she wishes she could do something else next year, but she's afraid to tell you. And it's affecting her at school."

Dad trades a look with Mom.

"Meaning what, exactly?" Mom asks.

Should I talk about how miserable Dahlia is? Maybe they don't want to hear that.

"I think she's having trouble with her math class. Other classes too." *Okay, no point stopping now.* "I know she's been spending a lot of time with this boy named Nico. He might be her boyfriend, I'm not sure. Anyway, they hang out after school sometimes."

Mom doesn't even ask for details. She jumps up and calls someone, possibly Sophie's mom again; I can barely hear her voice from the living room. A minute later her voice changes, like she's talking to someone different. Now she sounds loud and fake cheery. "Oh, how kind of you! Are you sure? Well, please don't rush, and sorry to disturb your dinner! Yes, us too! See you soon!"

She comes back to the kitchen. Her face looks almost human-colored, but behind her glasses her eyes are still too bright. "All right, so Dahlia's having supper at that boy's house—Nico. His dad says he'll drive her home as soon as they're finished."

"Nice of him," Dad says. He pushes away his plate. "She couldn't call to tell us that?"

"Apparently not." Mom shakes her head and does an exasperated laugh. "I don't know whether to hug her or ground her forever."

"Not a binary choice," Dad says. All of a sudden he looks exhausted. "Anything else we should know, Lyla? While we're on the subject?"

I shake my head.

I've already made Dahlia hate me forever, so really, there's nothing left to say.

PARALLEL UNIVERSE

I need to do something with myself until Dahlia gets home, so what I do is write in an old legal pad that Mom took from her office. Also, I use a black ballpoint pen, not my blue gel pen.

Switching it up, like Ms. Bowman said, I guess.

Not Chapter One, I write at the top of the page.

And I swear, I'm not even thinking about Ms. Bowman's other advice—*write your feelings, keep it personal.* But I find myself writing as Aster. From her point of view, in her voice.

UNSTUCK

Aster sat on a rock and thought: So what do I do now? How can I help my sister? One of Oleander's assistants (a low-ranking witch named Lousewort or Toadflax—I haven't decided) blabbed to me that the Vanguards aren't being held in a fancy castle but in a sort of giant tree house—in an enchanted tree (need a name!) as tall as a skyscraper!! So even though I tricked Oleander with that Milktooth, and somehow escaped the Defectors and the one-toed Beast, what do I do once I arrive at the tree house? It's really scary to climb that high, especially because the branches are sharp like daggers and full of prickly poison leaves!! Plus the tree house is guarded by vicious guard birds called Brownwings that fight off humans (rescuers and prisoners), so how do I convince Verbena to even TRY to escape? She's not an idiot—she'll definitely see the danger!!

Not only that: I'm sure Verbena will be furious that I told our parents about the Vanguard thing, even though I was only trying to rescue her! Will she listen to me now, or just dismiss me the way she usually does, like I'm just some silly little baby? Like I don't understand anything about this kingdom, and the way we're being forced into destinies like

Scribe and Vanguard? Will she accuse me of being jealous? Not caring about her feelings? What do I do if she won't even talk to me?

And if she does talk to me, and also listens to what I have to say, is it actually possible for me to save her from her fate? Because after all, I'm just a lowly Scribe without any skills or powers or magic. I don't even have a sword or a horse, because all Scribes get is paper and these terrible feather quill pens that leak ink all over your hands—

A car door slams.

I run over to my bedroom window. Dahlia is standing in our driveway, waving goodbye to someone inside a black SUV. She waits while the car pulls out of our driveway and takes off down the street. Then she takes a tissue out of her jacket pocket and blows her nose. After that she runs her hand through her beautiful hair, almost like she's about to go onstage.

I watch her slowly walk up the path to our house. Before she can take out her key, Mom and Dad are at the front door, throwing their arms around her, yelling. "How can you be so selfish, Dahlia? Didn't you think we'd be worried? Why didn't you communicate, or at least answer your phone? If Lyla hadn't told us . . ."

It's too upsetting to watch, too upsetting to hear. So I turn on my laptop and watch funny animal videos for a half hour.

When the house goes quiet, and I'm sure things have calmed down, I knock on Dahlia's door.

"Go away," she growls.

"Dahlia, please," I say in a small voice. "Can we just talk a second?"

"No, Lyla, we can't."

I open the door anyway. She's on her bed with Spumoni. Her face looks raw and her nose is pink, like she's been crying for the last few minutes.

"I'm sorry," I blurt.

"Yeah? For what?" Dahlia reaches into a cardboard box, pulls out a tissue, and honks her nose. "Ratting about where I was?"

"But Mom and Dad were really worried about you! So was I! And I *didn't* rat, Dahlia! How could I? I didn't even know where you were!"

"Well, you figured it out, obviously. Oh, and thanks for telling them I had a boyfriend. Because I *don't*."

"You don't? But I thought you and Nico—"

"Lyla, he's gay, all right? I may be in love with him, but we're just good friends." She takes another tissue. "Anyway, it's complicated, because he isn't out to his family, so it wasn't cool you told Mom and Dad we were dating. Now Nico's parents think so too, and that's not what he needed, all right?"

"*Oh.*" My heart is in my throat. "I'm so, so sorry, Dahlia!"

She dabs her eyes with the dirty tissue.

"But how come you didn't tell me this before?" My voice is shaking. "Because whenever I'd ask about him, you wouldn't answer. So *of course* I didn't know about Nico and his parents!"

"Well, you still shouldn't have *assumed* anything, all right? And speaking of parents"—Dahlia tosses the crumpled tissue across her bed—"I'm mad that you *also* told Mom and Dad I was failing math. And oh, by the way, don't want to go to college."

"Well, they need to know about that, don't they? They're paying this guy to help with your essay, and Mom's still freaking about the deadlines! But I bet if you tried to explain your feelings—"

She grabs another tissue. "They won't get it. Especially Mom."

"Dahlia, are you sure? Because they totally love you."

"It's not about love; it's about what they *expect* of me." She sniffs into her tissue. "And in case you were wondering, Lyla, the college thing wasn't your secret to tell."

"I know, but." I swallow hard. "Maybe I could help? I could talk to Mom and Dad for you. Or you could talk to them yourself, and I could be there to back you up—"

"No thanks. You've already done enough damage."

"Dahlia, please listen." Now I'm half begging, half crying. "I'm really sorry I told them all that stuff, okay? But I wasn't thinking straight. Because I was scared."

"Yeah? Of what?"

"No one knew where you were! You texted me you were in trouble, and then you stopped answering your phone. Even when Mom called."

"Well, maybe I was busy. I have a *life*; I'm not *always* on my stupid phone, you know."

"Okay, but you can't just text someone you're in trouble and then ignore them!" I wait a second. "So what kind of trouble did you mean?"

"Failed my calc test. Failing the class this quarter too." She throws the balled-up tissue toward her waste basket, missing by like a foot. "And anyway, I assumed whatever I told you would be *between us*. That you wouldn't go running to Mommy and Daddy. Because I thought I could trust you."

"And you can."

"Yeah, in a parallel universe where you're not jealous of me all the time."

I want to argue; I want to deny I'm jealous. But of course I can't, because I'm jealous of everyone lately: Stella, Rania, Dahlia—and Dahlia most of all, really. And does it mean I'm a terrible person? Who shouldn't have told Mom and Dad about Dahlia's math troubles, or my guess about where she was? Seriously, considering how scared and upset our parents were, did I even have a choice?

Although I also told them about the college thing. Probably Dahlia is right: I should have kept my mouth shut about that. Because it wasn't exactly relevant, and I did promise to keep it secret.

Why did I do that?

I really messed up, didn't I.

But maybe there's a way to make it okay?

Spumoni licks Dahlia's wet face. She's not even bothering to use a tissue anymore; she's just letting tears roll down her cheeks.

"Dahlia, please don't be mad," I say. "I swear I was only trying to—"

"You know what, Lyla? Don't even bother." Dahlia shoves Spumoni away and stares at her phone.

So it's clear that my sister has made up her mind about me, and there's no point arguing or defending myself or trying to undo the damage.

I leave her room and shut the door behind me.

PING-PONG

I barely sleep that night.

The next morning Dahlia isn't at the breakfast table. Dad is dressed for work, but Mom is in her treadmill clothes and red eyeglasses as she drinks her coffee.

"Aren't you going to work today?" I ask her.

She puts down her mug. "No, sweetie. Dahlia is taking a mental-health day, and I've decided to stick around too."

"Is she . . . okay?"

"Your sister needs a day off," Dad says. "Mom is meeting with Dahlia's school counselor later this morning."

"We have a lot to discuss." Mom rests her hand on mine. "Thanks for telling us what you did yesterday. I know you were in a difficult position, but you did the right thing by letting us know."

I shrug. Did I? I wish I could take back what I said, or just edit some of it.

Dad reads my mind. "You *absolutely* did the right thing, Ly," he says. "And now that we have a better understanding of the whole situation, we can try to help."

I nibble the crust of my toast. "So Dahlia talked to you about the college thing?"

"We started a conversation last night," Mom says. "There's a lot to consider."

Like what? I think but don't say.

Dad gets up from the table. He kisses my cheek, then Mom's. "Okay, off to the salt mines," he says.

Just as he's leaving, he locks eyes with Mom. "Let me know how it goes," he tells her as my stomach flips over.

All morning my brain is a Ping-Pong table. As soon as the ball lands on the Dahlia side of the table, smash. Now it's on the Rania side. And smash: now it's back to Dahlia. Smash again, back to Rania.

The score is close. I mean, I'm almost as upset about

Rania—whether we're even friends at all anymore—as I am about Dahlia. Although Dahlia wins because she's my sister, and because she's in actual trouble. And because part of it feels like my fault, no matter what Mom and Dad said at breakfast.

So even though we have a full-period test in Spanish and a pop quiz in science, I'm basically just watching the Ping-Pong ball zing back and forth. And by the time it's ELA, and Ms. Bowman tells us to take out our creative writing notebooks, what I want most is just to think about something else.

I decide to take my legal pad—not my writing notebook—to the library. As I'm leaving the classroom, I tell Ms. Bowman where I'm going.

She gives me a thumbs-up. "But today let's keep it to ten minutes, more or less," she says. "We need the rest of the period for reading groups."

I nod. *Ten minutes, more or less* is definitely a kind of time pressure. But with the contest deadline coming up, I can't just totally ignore the clock.

As soon as I arrive in the library, I notice Ms. Rosen teaching a group of sixth graders. She's saying the word "bibliography" in a non-library voice, and the kids are asking loud questions. Even so, I take the same table as yesterday, when Aster was telling off Elevator Guy. If I can tune out Dahlia and Rania, I can tune out these kids, I tell myself.

I flip the legal pad to a random page.

Not Chapter Two, I write with not-my-blue-gel-pen.

I approach the tree house where Verbena is a prisoner. (Although there needs to be some different name for this, because "tree house" sounds little-kid-ish, and this building is just scary, a prison with no windows. At least that's how it looks from the ground.)

How can I climb to the top without a rope or a knife?

I wish I had wings, or even shoes with good treads.

I wish I wasn't scared of heights.

I wish I was brave. But I guess sometimes you need to pretend you are, and that's almost the same thing.

COMPANY

Journey is humming as she spoons too much salsa on her burrito.

"So here's a question, Lyla," she says. "What animal would you want to ride into battle? Like if you could make any animal big enough to ride? I'm thinking a cassowary, because they can kick really hard, which adds a whole new battle capability."

"Yeah, let me think about that," I say. The truth is I'm not totally sure what a cassowary is. Some kind of giant bird, maybe? I definitely need to look it up.

As Journey bites into her burrito, I can see she's in a great mood, and I don't want to spoil it by telling her what happened yesterday when I tried to talk to Rania.

Instead I ask why she seems so happy.

"Oh, because I may be getting a new animal soon," she says.

"Really? You mean the sugar glider?" Right away I imagine Journey showing up to school with a small furry animal in a pouch, or maybe in her pocket. Would she keep it a secret from everyone but me? That would be cool, to know a secret creature.

"No, not the sugar glider," she says. "I read an article; apparently, they get depressed if you only get a single one. But my dad refuses to let me get two, so." She shrugs.

"Oh. I'm sorry, Journey."

"Why are you apologizing?"

"I'm not. I just mean I'm sorry that you can't get a sugar glider. Since you said you wanted one."

"Eh, that's okay, Lyla. I really just want my animals to be happy." Journey takes a bite of burrito. "Anyhow, I'm getting something even better now. Wanna guess what?"

"No idea. A cassowary?"

"A hedgehog!"

"Wait, you *are*?" My voice is too loud; Noah looks up

at me from a few tables away. So now I whisper: "But are hedgehogs inside pets? I mean, *animals*."

"Sure they are! And I bet you're confusing them with porcupines. It's a common error."

Just then, for some strange reason, Stella sits down at our table. I know I have to change the subject fast, because I can't imagine Stella discussing sugar gliders versus hedgehogs or hedgehogs versus porcupines, or anything else Journey wants to talk about. And after that conversation with Rania, I don't want Stella also deciding that Journey is "weird."

Before I can even think of anything, Stella says, "Hey, Lyla. What happened to you in ELA?"

"Nothing," I say. "I just went to the library. Ms. Bowman lets me go write there if I want. And I think it's helping a little."

"You do? That's great," Stella says, not even sarcastically. "Well, I still volunteer to give feedback. If you ever want."

"Thanks." I glance at Journey, who Stella has been ignoring again. And I think about the cassowary comment, how Journey has all these amazing ideas. So maybe . . . she could help for real?

"But Journey already offered, remember?" I tell Stella.

"And actually, Journey, I was going to ask if you were available after school today. To read my story," I add, in case she wasn't following.

"Me?" Journey blinks.

"Yeah, I haven't written very much, but—"

"Oh, sure, Lyla. I'll read it. If you want."

"I really do," I say. And as I hear myself saying this, I'm sure it's the truth.

At dismissal I wait in the hallway for Journey. I watch her grab a notebook from her locker, then slam the door without talking to anyone, and without anyone talking to her. All around her kids are joking and laughing, talking about what they're doing after school, and it makes me sad how separate and alone she seems.

It's really so unfair. Just because back in fifth grade some nasty kids decided Journey was "weird," why is that what people *still* think about her? I'm not saying *I* didn't think she was weird at first, but that was before I got to know her.

Seriously, it's like once people *expect* you to be weird, nothing you do or say will change their minds.

Suddenly Dahlia's words flash in my brain: *It's not about love; it's about what they expect.* And I guess if you're a superstar like Dahlia, people *expect* you to win every contest, get perfect grades, go to a fancy college, even if that's not who you really are. Maybe if you're Journey, people *expect* you to have no friends, so then, abracadabra, you don't.

What would it be like if people *didn't* expect stuff, didn't assign words like "superstars" or "weirdos"? "Jocks" and "brains" also.

Vanguards and Scribes, too, actually.

Words that get you stuck, and decide your fate forever. Unless someone rescues you. Or you escape.

"Hey, Lyla, you ready?" Journey asks as she zips her jacket.

I nod. For a second I consider inviting her to my house—but no, that would be impossible today. Because I'm sure my house is a war zone, with yelling and slamming doors and tears. Not exactly a place for quiet reading, and definitely not a place to bring a friend.

So I suggest we go to the small park about two blocks from school, and right away Journey agrees.

SIDEKICK

By the time we pick out a bench, I'm thinking this is a big mistake.

I mean, my writing pad is almost empty. What made me decide I was ready to show it to anyone? If Stella hadn't offered to read my story, I wouldn't have even mentioned it to Journey. And now here we are, and she expects to see chapters. Maybe not a finished book, but something a little further along.

"I don't have a whole lot," I admit as I take the pad out of my backpack. "Just a few pages. We also have a writing notebook, but we're supposed to leave that in the classroom. I deleted most of it, anyway."

Journey's eyes get big. "How come?"

"I told you, remember? Everything I wrote sucked."

"Your *teacher* said that?"

"Ms. Bowman? Of course not! She'd never use a word like 'sucked.'"

"But you would? Why?"

"Because it's my story. So I'm allowed to hate it."

"I guess." Journey tilts the brim of her cap. "Well, Lyla, I'm not any kind of writing expert. But you can show me if you want."

I flip to the pages I wrote in the library today. "Here," I say, putting the pad in Journey's lap.

"You have good handwriting," she says politely. "Better than mine."

"Yeah, well. This is just a rough draft. I'll type another version for the writing contest."

As Journey reads, she hums softly. I try to watch a pigeon on the grass pecking what looks like a pretzel, but the whole time my heart is banging, and I can't help peeking whenever she turns a page.

Why am I doing this? My story isn't ready. Probably it never will be.

She's going to think I'm a talentless idiot. Also a fake. Maybe she's right about that too!

And she told me she doesn't read fantasy a whole lot anyway. So I doubt she'll say anything useful. Probably just something vague and nice, so she doesn't hurt my feelings.

I should have shown it to Noah instead, because he's a big reader. But he said he thought it would be "amazing," and what if he didn't like it? Or just compared my story with Orion's?

Too bad I can't show Rania. Or talk to Rania. Or anything.

Although maybe Rania isn't the right person either.

Maybe she never was.

Suddenly Journey looks up at me.

"Lyla, this is going to be very good," she says slowly.

"You really think so?"

"Uh-huh. I really like the plot about the Vanguards, how they think they're so special but they don't realize they're in danger. Also it's cool that a Scribe has to save a Vanguard. And she can't use magic or anything, just her brain."

Whoa. This is exactly what my story is about, and someone gets it! Even from just a few pages!

Journey scratches her nose. "But I think I caught a typo. Not that it's typed."

"You mean there's a mistake? Where?"

She flips between two pages. "Here you call the sister

Verbena Hyacinth, but here it's Hyacinth Verbena."

"That's just because I haven't decided what to name her yet."

"Well, I prefer the name Verbena, if you're asking. And is Milktooth supposed to be a real stone?"

"No; I just made it up." I take a breath. "The story is that a witch named Oleander bribes Aster to find a gem called Cloudstone in order to pass through the Quagmire. But Aster tricks her with a nugget of Milktooth instead. Which basically neutralizes all of Oleander's spells."

"Yeah, I got all that, Lyla. But how does Aster even know about the Milktooth?"

"Her tutor told her once. He's called the Seer."

"Okay, but I don't get why he'd even talk about it to a Scribe. And I don't understand how Aster would recognize Milktooth but Oleander wouldn't. Because Oleander is this powerful witch, so how is she fooled?"

Erg, she's right. I didn't think of that. "Journey, just because she's powerful doesn't mean she knows *everything*."

Journey shrugs. "And something else: Why does Juniper keep calling her Aster if she doesn't remember anything from before she became a Defector? Shouldn't she not even recognize her?"

Now my face is starting to sweat. "Okay, yeah. I'll fix that."

"And why does the Beast have only one toe?"

"*Why?* There isn't a reason; he just does!"

"Well, I think you need more description about it."

"About the *toe*?"

"Yeah. It's really interesting."

Wait, seriously? I definitely agree with her other comments, but I'm not so sure about the toe.

I'm ready to end this conversation when Journey adds: "But I really like Aster's personality. She reminds me of me."

What?

I'm so shocked I almost laugh.

Of everything I've been expecting Journey to say, this was the absolute bottom of the list. No—it wasn't even *on* the list.

"That's incredible," I tell her. "Because actually, Aster is based on *me*."

"She is?"

I nod. "When I was blocked, Ms. Bowman told me to write my feelings. And I think it helped with Aster's character."

"Cool cool." Journey runs her fingers through her bangs.

"What I meant is that Aster's in her own head a lot, right? My mom always says that's how I am, too. So I was thinking if . . ." She stops.

"If what?"

"I don't know. You really want to hear?"

"Of course I do, Journey! That's why I'm showing it to you!"

"Okay, so. All we get is what Aster's thinking, so maybe it would be better if Aster had someone else to talk to, like a sidekick or something. Even someone to argue with."

I don't say anything.

"And maybe this person could go with her through the Quagmire. And then they could team up to fight the Beast and the—what were they called again?"

"The Defectors."

"Right. That would be more fun to read. In my opinion."

I chew my lip.

"Okay," I say after a few seconds, "but the story is supposed to be about Aster and her sister. It's already pretty complicated; I'm not sure I want to add another major character!"

"Never mind. It was just a suggestion." Her face pinches. "Are you mad at me, Lyla?"

"Of course not," I say as I slip the pad into my backpack. "I'm just thinking about what you said. You're the only one who's given me feedback, Journey. Who I've asked to, I mean. So thanks."

Even though she pulls down the brim of her cap, I can tell she's smiling.

SECOND THOUGHT

After this conversation I have this strong urge to go and write. But with all the Dahlia business at home, I also want to stay away as long as possible.

So I convince Journey to hang out a little longer. We walk around the park a few times, counting the pigeons. She tells me about some article she read—how hedgehogs are lactose intolerant.

"So that means no ice cream for them," I say. "And no pizza, either. I guess I'd make a terrible hedgehog."

"Yeah, me too." Then she starts talking about how

when a hedgehog smells or tastes something strong, it covers itself in saliva. "Same as a cat licking itself," she says. "It's called *self-anointing*. Isn't that a great word?"

I nod. It's really so cool how Journey does all this research. Also how she likes words like "self-anointing."

I'm only one-third listening, though. Now I'm wondering about a sidekick for Aster. Because okay, I admit it—at first I totally rejected Journey's idea. But the more I think about it, the more a sidekick makes sense. Aster really *does* need someone to take her out of her head a little. Otherwise the whole book will just be one long monologue—except for the fight with Hyacinth/Verbena, and the chapters about Oleander and Juniper. And of course the big battle scenes.

All right, but what *sort* of sidekick should Aster have? Another Scribe? That could work, I guess.

Maybe the other Scribe could be a boy Aster likes? No, because it's not that type of story! I always hate it when just because a book is about a boy and a girl, it's like there has to be some kind of romance. And anyway, my story needs some kind of conflict, even if the characters are working together to save the Vanguards.

How about a boy Aster thinks she hates—until the ending, when they become friends?

Hmm, maybe. But the friendship can't be too predictable. And why does it have to be a boy at all? Aster's sidekick could be a girl, right? Or someone nonbinary? Or someone she doesn't even think of as a friend. And the sidekick doesn't even have to be a *person*. It could be a magical creature, as long as the creature talks. No point adding a sidekick with zero dialogue.

Ooh, I like that! A talking magical creature! Maybe like a horse Aster can ride sometimes?

Eh, no. Forget that. A talking horse is babyish.

Better to stick to a human kid, another Scribe. Then it could be like: *Revolt of the Scribes! Scribes to the Rescue!*

In a kingdom ruled by royalty and Vanguards, lowly Scribes rise up to save the day!

"Is that what you think, Lyla?" Journey is saying. "Should I *not* put the hedgehog's cage in my bedroom?"

I blink. "I'm actually . . . not sure."

"Because here's the problem: I know the hedgehog will be nervous the first few days in my house, and it'll be easier for us to bond if we're in the same room. But hedgehogs are nocturnal, *extremely* active overnight, and if she's scuffling around in her cage, I won't get any sleep."

"Yeah," I say. "Although will you get any sleep if you're separated, and worried about her?"

"Probably not," she admits. And then she grins.

And now, for some reason I don't even get, I'm grinning too.

SURRENDER

Hello?" I call as I step inside our house.

The kitchen is empty, and weirdly quiet. An empty raspberry yogurt container is in the sink, the only clue that anyone is home. But it's just one container, and out of all of us, only Mom likes raspberry.

I walk into the living room, barely breathing. Mom is sitting on the sofa talking on her phone. "Oh yes, I agree completely," she's saying. "But what are the options at this point?"

I wave.

"One sec," she says to Whoever. She rests her phone on the sofa seat. "Hey, sweetie. I'm talking to Dad. How was school?"

"Fine. I was hanging out with Journey just now. That's why I'm late."

"Okay. You should have texted, though."

"Sorry. I'm not used to you being home after school." I take a breath. "So . . . how's it going? I mean with Dahlia."

"Progress, I think. We're both taking a breather at the moment. But at least we're talking."

"Where is she?"

"In her room. Okay, Ly, let me finish this call now."

I climb the stairs, my heart banging. What should I do if Dahlia's door is closed? If I knock, she'll tell me to go away. But I have this feeling that I need to talk to her. Not that I have anything specific to say, really.

I throw my backpack on my bed. Then I walk down the hall to Dahlia's room.

Her door is open.

I take a step inside. She's on her bed with her laptop. Spumoni is curled up by her naked feet.

I clear my throat. "Hi," I say.

"Oh. Hi," she says. Dahlia's face is pale and puffy. Her hair is unbrushed, flat, and greasy—a shock, if you know my sister. And she's still in what she wears for pj's—an ancient Pokémon tee and track shorts.

"What's going on?" I ask.

"With what?"

"I don't know. You took today off from school, right? Are you okay?"

"Never better." She rolls her eyes. "I've surrendered, so."

"What does that mean?"

She throws her bare legs across the bed. "Well, after Mom and I had a long 'conversation,' I spent the morning finishing my college essay. And the way my grades are going this semester, there's no point applying to my top schools anymore. So now I'm working on my safeties."

"Safeties?"

"Schools that might possibly still want me. They used to be safe bets, but not now, I guess. Anyway, I'm almost done with one application, so woohoo."

I sit on the edge of her bed. "Dahlia, why are you doing this?"

"Doing what?"

"Applying to colleges. If you really don't want to go, I mean."

She shuts her laptop. "Well, maybe I'm just tired of fighting with everyone all the time. Especially Mom."

Should I keep going? Even if she gets mad at me all over again?

What am I doing here if I'm too scared to help?

"Listen, Dahlia," I say carefully, "you really *don't* have to do this, you know? Even if it's what everyone expects."

She shrugs helplessly. "Yeah?"

"Definitely! Come on, you're the smartest person I know! Just do whatever you want! I mean, it's your life, right?"

At that very moment, Spumoni farts in his sleep. It doesn't make a sound, but the stink fills the bedroom.

"Eww," I say, grinning.

Dahlia doesn't grin back, but her mouth twitches a little at the corners.

I choose to take it as a sign. "Can I ask you something? If you could do anything in the world, anything you wanted for the next year, what would it be?"

"I don't know," she says. "Maybe travel?"

"Like where?"

"South America? I've always wanted to go to Peru and see Machu Picchu. And I'm still doing okay in Spanish. That's my one decent grade this semester."

"Okay, cool! So maybe—"

"Nah." She hugs her knees.

"Why not?"

"Because Mom and Dad have been saving for college since I was a baby. I'm sure they won't let me spend all that money on sightseeing."

"Yeah, maybe not," I admit.

We sit there for a minute or two while Dahlia flops Spumoni's ears.

Then I say, "Okay, so what if you got a job somewhere, like in another country? And went to college afterward, if that's what you really want?"

My sister sighs. "How would I even *get* a job in another country? Anyway, Mom and Dad wouldn't let me."

"How do you know?"

"Because I've lived with them for seventeen years. Five more than you."

"Yeah, I know, you're great at math. You don't need to show off, Dahlia." I stick out my tongue at her, but she doesn't even react. "Seriously, though, Mom and Dad love you, right? So they want you to be happy. And I bet if you explained—"

"Omigod, Lyla. You're saying I should have another *conversation*?"

"It doesn't have to be horrible. You want me to go with you? To talk to them?"

UNSTUCK

Dahlia scratches an invisible mosquito bite on her elbow. "No point, because I know *exactly* what'll happen. They'll just say: 'Okay, but what's your plan? Get on a plane? And hope a job is waiting for you when you land?'"

"Come on, I bet there's a way to make it happen. There's got to be! You're not stuck, Dahlia." Saying that word—*stuck*—makes me wince a little, but I say it anyway.

She sighs. "I don't know, Ly. Maybe there *isn't* a way. But thanks."

"For what?"

"Trying." She gives me a small, tired smile.

We watch as Spumoni stretches, jumps off the bed, and leaves the bedroom.

"Hey, can you take him outside to pee?" she says. "I need to talk to Nico now."

I know it's her way of getting rid of me, but this time I don't argue.

RESCUE

"What are you doing here, Aster?"

"I've come to rescue you, Verbena! With my sidekick X!"

"Rescue me? From what?"

"It's too long and complicated to explain right now. But you need to trust me. Please let me help you!"

"Aster, I'm fine. I don't need any help. Anyway, it's too late. My fate is sealed."

"Wait. You mean you know what happens to Vanguards??"

"I do now," she replied sadly. "But I'm powerless to stop it."

Even though when I came home my plan was to write a sidekick subplot for Aster, I can't stop thinking about Dahlia. I write my story for about twenty minutes; then I switch over to doing research.

I'm still on my laptop an hour later, when Mom calls us downstairs for dinner. By now I have an idea—but what should I do with it? This is going to be extremely tricky. Of course I don't want Dahlia to get mad at me all over again. But if I keep my mouth shut, if I don't even *try* to help, she'll just let herself be trapped. Forced into something she doesn't want to do, something that will make her stressed-out and miserable, because that's what people *expect*.

I have to save her. Have to at least try.

I wash my hands and go downstairs to supper.

"Well, today sounds very productive," Dad is saying as the four of us eat stir-fried chicken and veggies. "Dahlia, Mom says you already submitted the early-decision application?"

"Uh-huh." She pokes her food with a chopstick.

"And tonight you'll work on another application? Just in case?"

"Not sure."

Mom and Dad trade a look.

I kick Dahlia's shin under the table.

She looks at me with empty eyes.

My cue, I tell myself.

"Yeah, so we were talking," I say loudly.

Dad eats some rice. "About what?"

I try to catch Dahlia's eye again, but she's stabbing a snow pea.

"Taking a year off," I say. My voice is still too loud, but so what. "Getting a job and traveling. And then going to college afterward, if that's what Dahlia wants."

I kick her again, even harder this time.

She throws me a helpless look.

Talk, I mouth at her. *Go.*

"Yeah," Dahlia finally says. She rests her chopsticks on her napkin. "I mean, it's *probably* what I want. What I *will* want. But right now . . ." Her shoulders shoot up to her ears, then slump. "The whole college thing just feels *wrong* to me. Like a big waste of time. And money."

"But I thought we agreed—" Mom begins.

"Yeah, we did," Dahlia says. "But after that I talked to Lyla."

"Lyla?" Both my parents are staring at me now. Like: *What do you have to do with this?*

"One sec," I say as I type something into my phone. Then I hand my phone to Dahlia. It's open to a website called WorkSeeSouthAmerica. "Check this out. It's in Peru. They give you a job teaching English during the week, and on weekends they take you sightseeing. To Machu Picchu, and other places!"

Dahlia starts clicking around. "Oh wow," she says. "Omigod, Lyla. It's absolutely perfect!"

Mom and Dad both look stunned.

"This is for high school graduates?" Dad asks doubtfully.

"Yep," I say as Dahlia keeps clicking. "It's a gap-year program, for kids to do before college. They list other jobs too, but most of them are teaching. It's not just sightseeing! And Dahlia could earn money while she's there."

Dahlia's smile is beautiful. She looks like Dahlia again. "Can I do this? It's just for one year! Please? Please?"

Mom and Dad have an eye conversation.

"We'll need to look into this first," Mom answers slowly. "We're not just shipping you off to some foreign country."

"There's a lot to research," Dad says. "We're not saying yes."

"But you're not saying no!" Dahlia jumps up and throws her arms around them both. "Thank you so, so much!"

"We haven't agreed to anything yet, baby," Dad warns.

"But you're considering it, right? Omigod, I need to call Nico." She's just about to run out of the kitchen, but then she stops.

"Thank you, Lyla," she says.

"No problem," I answer, grinning.

DEADLINE

"Who are you?"

"My name is Safari."

"That's a weird name. But it's nice."

"Thank you. It's probably the wrong name for a Scribe, though. Because all we do is sit at our desks the whole day."

"You're a Scribe? I've never seen you before."

"I just received my assignment. To be honest, I'm disappointed, because it's not my true talent."

"What's your true talent, then?"

"Communicating with magical creatures. Although I've never tried with the ones that live in the Quagmire. Like the one-toed Beast."

I thought about this. Should I invite Safari on my quest? I barely knew her!!!

But maybe she could help me navigate through the Quagmire—even if she couldn't communicate with the Beast.

It would definitely be less lonely and scary to travel with another person. Although would Safari agree to come with me? Why would she? The Quagmire was extremely dangerous!

And who knew what would happen once we got to the other side?

Now that Aster has a sidekick, I can't stop writing. That's the good news.

The bad news is that these scenes keep popping into my head at the worst times, like when I'm in math, or when I'm outside walking Spumoni.

Also, they're in a totally random order. So even though I write them as soon as I can, now I have a pad with a whole bunch of scenes that aren't connected in a way that makes sense. So I definitely can't submit these chapters to the writing contest! I mean, even if I tear out all the pages in my pad and arrange them in chronological order, there are still these Quagmire-sized holes in the plot.

And now I can't even work on my story during ELA, because we've switched to persuasive essays. Just like Ms. Bowman promised, we don't have to write exactly five paragraphs—but I still think they're incredibly boring.

We've been doing these essays for more than a week when Ms. Bowman asks me to stay after class. I wait until everyone leaves the room, then walk over to her desk.

"So, Lyla, I wanted to check in with you," she says, smiling a little. "How's the writing going?"

"Okay, I guess," I say. "I'm finishing Why Audiobooks Are Just As Good As Print Books. But I still need a conclusion."

She folds her hands. "Ah. Well, I'm sure you'll come up with something! But what I really meant was: How's your story coming along?"

"Better, actually," I admit. "I showed it to my friend Journey and she said Aster needed a sidekick, like another Scribe to go with her through the Quagmire. After she said that, I wrote a lot."

"Oh, Lyla, that's fantastic!" Ms. Bowman's face is glowing. "I'm really glad you shared your writing with a friend! Talking always, always helps."

"Yeah, but." I shrug. "I can't submit it to the contest."

"Why not?"

"Because all I have is a bunch of random scenes. The judges won't understand what they're reading!"

"Hmm," Ms. Bowman says slowly. "Well, Lyla, I just think it's great that you're moving ahead with your story. Even if you *don't* end up submitting to the contest."

I guess she sees something in my face, because right away she adds, "Although I wonder if there's a way you could explain the action to the judges. Maybe add a note to put the scenes in context?"

"Maybe. But I don't want to write a whole *essay* about it."

"No, of course not. Hmm. Is there something else you can submit instead? A poem, perhaps?"

I think about this. But the only poem I ever wrote was back in fourth grade, a haiku about Spumoni:

> *Lazy old brown dog,*
>
> *Why do you fart in your sleep?*
>
> *Do you dream of treats?*

I shake my head.

"The reason I'm asking, Lyla, is that the deadline is coming up very soon. *If* you're submitting. But it's completely okay if you've changed your mind."

I don't answer.

Because . . . is it even possible to meet that deadline?

I mean, without totally freaking out?

INTERSECTION

At lunch Journey can't stop talking about her hedgehog. She got it last night—a young male African pygmy, small enough to fit in her hand.

"He's got the sweetest little face," she says. "I'm naming him Nigel."

"Nigel?" I'm not in a smiling mood, but I smile at this anyway. "That's such a great name! Why did you pick it?"

"I don't know! He just sort of told me that's his name." She grins. "Want to come over after school to meet him?"

I explain that I'd love to—and seriously, I would—but I

need to work on my story if I'm going to make the deadline.

She takes a huge bite of burrito. "Can I ask you something, Lyla? Why do you care about that contest so much?"

"I don't know," I say. "My sister won second place when she was in middle school. And—"

"—you want to beat her?"

The way she says this makes me cringe. Like she thinks I'm in some kind of track competition with Dahlia. A track *meet*, I mean.

I eat the crust off my cheese sandwich.

"Sorry if I offended you," Journey says.

"You didn't offend me," I reply.

Still, it's a relief when she's back to talking about Nigel the hedgehog.

Noah catches up to me as I walk home that afternoon.

"Hey, Lyla," he says, a little out of breath. "You going over to Dickinson? So am I."

It takes me a second to realize what he's talking about.

"Actually, I'm just walking home," I say.

"Oh."

Is he disappointed? He kind of sounds that way.

"Yeah," I say, "I had a fight with my friend. So I might not be going there anymore."

"You mean Rania?"

I look at him. "How did you—"

"Orion told me. He heard Rania talking about it the other day. He pays attention because . . . I dunno, I think he likes her."

"Everyone likes Rania."

"No, I mean *likes* her."

It's not like I didn't figure this out on my own—but even so, it feels weird to hear Noah say it. Another reminder that Rania is talking about me at school. Also that she isn't talking *to* me. Because it used to be that when Rania was in a crush situation, she'd tell me about it nonstop. Tell me *herself*.

I shove my hands into the front pockets of Dahlia's old sweatshirt. Should I say anything else? There's no reason not to. I mean, if Rania and I aren't even friends now.

"Although some of her friends aren't too nice," I say.

"You mean Maeve?"

I peek at him. "You know her?"

"She was in my class like since kindergarten. Her and Gracie."

Noah's voice gets tight and he's looking at the pavement. So I get the feeling he's uncomfortable admitting this, like maybe he knows something awful.

And now I have no choice but to keep going. "Can I ask you a question, Noah? Did you ever see Maeve and Gracie—and Ayana, too—bully anyone?"

Noah pauses. "I guess you're asking about Journey."

"Yes, I am. Exactly."

"Well, everyone saw. Not so much with Ayana, but those other two . . . yeah. It got pretty bad."

We walk half a block without talking, until we get to a busy intersection.

The traffic light is red, so now we have to wait.

"It's so unfair," I announce. "I see people *still* avoiding Journey, like she's contagious or something. But she's actually just smart and nice."

"I guess," he says. "I mean, I know her but I don't really *know* her."

"Well, maybe you should." Then I shock myself. "You could eat lunch with us sometime. If you wanted."

"Oh. Thanks." Okay, he's definitely embarrassed. "Well, I need to turn here if I'm going to Dickinson."

"See you, Noah," I say, wondering if I will.

BEST FRIENDS

"Safari, I'd like you to meet Ezra."

Safari looks at him like she isn't too enthusiastic. "We already know each other, Aster. We were in Scribe training together."

"Right, I forgot that. So anyway, I was thinking Ezra could join us on our mission to rescue Verbena."

"Why?" Safari rolls her eyes. "Because the more the merrier?"

"No, because safety in numbers. And Ezra has great ideas for getting through the Quagmire."

*"But I won't come if you feel weird about it,"
Ezra tells her.*

*She scowls. "It's fine, as long as you don't
interfere with my work."*

*"What's she talking about?" Ezra whispers as
Safari walks off to pack her satchel. "What work?"*

*"You don't know?" I whisper back. "She
communicates with magical creatures. It's her
superpower."*

*Ezra looks confused. "So if she has a superpower,
how come she got assigned Scribe?"*

"How come any of us did?" I answer.

By five o'clock I've written eight more pages—nothing
for the contest, but I'm happy anyway. Because now Aster
has other characters to interact with. And Journey was right:
it's much more interesting than just Aster's thoughts, over
and over and over. Plus, Ezra and Safari can play off each
other—maybe have a bit of conflict, although in a good way.

I'm in the kitchen eating chips when Dahlia shows up
with Sophie.

"There she is, our hero!" Sophie shouts. "The best little
sister ever!"

I have to smile. "What are you talking about?"

"Dahlia says you found an awesome program for her?" Sophie says. "In Peru?"

"I just did a little research. That's all."

"It's not little, it's major!" My sister's face is glowing; she definitely looks like Dahlia again. "This gap-year thing is *perfect*! I don't know why no one told me about it before! Or why I didn't think of it myself!"

"Because you needed your genius baby sister, that's why," Sophie says, making a kissy face at me.

"I'm not a baby," I pretend growl.

"Oh, sure, of course you're not," Dahlia says. She sticks out her tongue at me.

Then the two of them grab my hands and we twirl around the kitchen like we're doing ring-around-the-rosy in hyperspeed.

Suddenly we stop, laughing and panting, as the room keeps spinning.

"Omigod," Dahlia says. She grabs the counter. "I think I'm going to barf."

"Don't say that," Sophie says. "Don't even think about it!"

My sister takes a few deep breaths. "I'll try, Soph. I'm probably just freaking because I want it so much! What if Mom and Dad say I can't go?"

"They won't!" Sophie shouts. "You're *absolutely* going to Peru, and I'll come visit you on winter break!"

"Seriously?"

"I'll have to! Because I'll miss my bestie too much!"

They throw their arms around each other in a big hug.

It's hard to watch. I mean, I'm happy for my sister because she seems like Dahlia again. I'm also happy that she has Sophie for a best friend.

But I can't help thinking about Rania, the way she used to hug me all the time.

The way the two of us used to be.

And it feels like someone punched me in the chest.

TOUGHER

At dinner Mom and Dad are talking about politics while Dahlia is busy relocating her spaghetti, pushing it from one side of her plate to the other without eating very much.

Just as Dad dumps half a bottle of ranch dressing all over his salad, she puts down her fork. "So can we please talk about this gap-year thing?" she begs. "I mean if you found out anything about that Peru program? And decided if I can go?"

Mom and Dad trade a look.

"Sure we can," Dad says. "We were just waiting for the

right moment. Lyla, you're ready to clear your plate now?"

"You mean you want me to leave the table?" I ask loudly.

He blinks. "Well, we have lots to discuss here, sweet-heart. Don't you have homework . . . ?"

"Lyla should stay," Dahlia says, meeting my eyes. "Okay?" I nod.

"All right, so," Mom says. She takes a sip of water and wipes her mouth with a napkin. "Here's where we are, Dahlia. I've spent all day researching, and also talking to your school counselor. I've also chatted with several other parents she put me in touch with whose kids have done similar programs. And I have to tell you that Dad and I are not sure this Peru program is the best fit."

Dahlia's face crumples. "It's *not*? What's wrong with it?"

"Nothing's *wrong* with it," Dad says. I can tell he's choos-ing his words carefully. "It sounds wonderful in many ways. But it's very far away. And very expensive. And it doesn't have much educational content, as far as we can tell."

"Okay, but if I'm not going to college—"

"Hold on," Mom cuts in. "Dahlia, we thought the idea was that you'd do some sort of program that would get you ready to enroll in college the year after. So we'll still need that money for your education, won't we?"

"We're very sorry, baby," Dad says. "But the Peru

program sounds almost like a vacation, with a few hours of work thrown in. It's really not what we had in mind."

I peek at Dahlia, expecting her to burst into tears or start shouting or at least argue.

But here's what she does: nothing.

"Although possibly there are *other* programs—" Mom begins.

Dahlia shakes her head. "Never mind," she says, in a flat, not-Dahlia voice. "I knew it was too good to be true."

Then she gets up and leaves the table.

After that conversation at the dinner table it doesn't even occur to me to work on my story, even with the deadline coming fast. Because how can I abandon my sister now? I can't.

I knock on her door. "Dahlia? Can I come in?"

"What for," she says.

I open the door anyway. "If you want to yell at me, go ahead."

I say this even though she looks the opposite of mad. In fact, I wish she did look mad. Not just faded and blurry, like someone drew her with a smudgy pencil.

"Lyla, what do you want?" she asks, not even looking up from her phone.

"Just listen to me, okay? I really don't get why you're

acting like this! Because you told Sophie you wanted a gap year more than anything, right? So if that's true, you should fight for it!"

"Yeah, well, I already told you I'm sick of fighting. And anyway, there's no point."

"Sure there is! Mom and Dad didn't say you couldn't do *any* gap-year program, just that one in Peru. So maybe if we find another one—"

"We'll just get my hopes up again, and then they'll say they hate that program too."

For a few seconds I don't know what to do. I mean, Dahlia has always been the Superstar Student. It's not like she didn't work hard this whole time—more like she knew that as long as she *did* work hard, she'd definitely ace all her classes. So maybe she's just not used to struggling, or fighting for what she really wants.

And I guess I'm . . . the opposite? Because all the time I freaked about my writing, I never gave up, did I.

For the first time in my life I feel stronger than my big sister. No, not stronger: tougher.

"Okay," I say, trying to keep my voice calm. "So we need to find a program that's really cool, but with more educational stuff, and not as far away. Because it doesn't *have* to be Peru, right?"

"I guess not," she says. "But I don't know any other programs."

"Right, so let's research! I'll help. We'll do it together."

"Errrgghhh," Dahlia says. But she doesn't argue.

I get my laptop, and we sit on her bed reading websites and testimonials, taking notes, and searching maps. After a few minutes Spumoni jumps up on the bed, licks Dahlia's face, plops on her legs, and begins snoring. It's a peaceful sound, even though it reminds me of a rusty old lawn mower.

We're like this for almost an hour when Mom pokes her head into the room. I can tell she's surprised to see me here.

"What's going on, girls?" she asks.

I peek at Dahlia. She pops her eyes at me like, *You tell her, okay?* So I admit what we're doing.

It's not like I expect Mom to start arguing or lecturing or explaining why we're wasting our time. Even so, I don't expect to see her smile.

"Yes, Dad and I are looking for programs too," she says. "There's so much to read; it's a bit overwhelming! But can I share what we've found?"

I look at Dahlia.

"Why not," she says, shrugging.

ESCAPE

At breakfast the next morning, Dahlia can't stop bab-
bling.

After I went to bed last night, she says, the three of
them—Mom, Dad, and Dahlia—kept researching gap-year
programs, narrowing it down to Costa Rica, Canada, and
Mexico. None of these programs is exactly cheap, but they
all have six-month and three-month options, which means
they wouldn't be as expensive as a whole year in Peru.

"Although to help pay for it I'll have to get a job when I
get back," Dahlia says as she chomps on her toast. "Maybe

babysit or work in a grocery store or something? But it'll totally be worth it!"

"Yeah, definitely." I grin. "Do you have a first choice?"

"Oh, Costa Rica! It's all about sustainability! And the ecosystem! Omigod, Lyla, you get to protect sea-turtle eggs from predators! On the beach! Doesn't that sound *amazing*? Of course, Mom and Dad still need to talk to a bunch of people before they agree to anything. *And* I had to promise I'd finish my other college applications by the end of today. But—"

"Wait, why do you need to apply to college? I mean, if you're not going next year."

"Oh, so I can go the year after!"

"But I thought—"

"Lyla, I'm pretty sure I'll *want* to go, if I can just clear my head and de-stress first. It's called deferring admission; plenty of kids do it! But for my top choice tomorrow's the deadline, so."

Suddenly it hits me: tomorrow is the contest deadline too. But even if I had an idea what to write—a short action-packed chapter that doesn't need maps or family trees or a whole essay to explain the story—when would I write it? Today is going to be a nightmare, with a Spanish test I haven't studied for, plus another math quiz. Maybe I can try to sneak-write during my other classes, but it won't be easy.

"Well, I'm really happy for you," I tell Dahlia as I get up from the table.

"Don't be happy *yet*," she replies. But she's beaming.

Are you ready to go, Verbena?

As ready as I'll ever be, I guess.

Okay, so here's the plan. Safari will distract the Brownwings, while Ezra stands guard on the ground. You and I will climb down the tree—

But wait! What if someone sees me when I get down?

You'll wear my extra Scribe uniform. Here—put it on fast!

I will. Aster?

Yes?

Thank you for saving me. You're a good sister.

Don't thank me yet! Let's get you out of here first.

By ELA I've scribbled something, but it's extremely rough, in no shape to submit to the contest. Also, it's a *chapter in a novel*—so even if I polish it up, fill in all the blanks, it won't have a beginning/middle/ending.

Now I'm starting to feel that icy sort of writing panic again.

So it's like I have no choice. At the start of the period I ask Ms. Bowman if I can go to the library. I remind her about the contest deadline, and promise to make up any work I miss.

She doesn't seem enthusiastic. "Lyla, you know how I feel about that contest," she says quietly. "And it's not more important than our class time together."

But I guess when she sees the look on my face, she changes her mind.

"All right," she says, sighing.

"Thank you. *A lot*," I say.

I wait for her to crinkle her eyes at me, but she doesn't.

I run out of the classroom anyway.

KRAZY GLUE

Verbena and I are sloshing through the Quagmire
with Ezra and Safari.

> *The four of us are sloshing through the Quagmire*
> *when all of a sudden we spy the one-toed Beast.*

> *We are sloshing when suddenly—*

> *We're sloshing. And suddenly—*

My hands are making tiny puddles on the pages of my
notebook. Everything I write is a smeary blur, even the
words I've crossed out.

What's wrong with me, anyway? I was making so much progress, and now it feels like I'm stuck all over again!

Uggghhh.

I hate this story.

I hate *writing* this story.

But also *not* writing this story.

And by now I'm thinking that any version of it, even a not-so-complicated chapter from the very beginning, would be totally wrong for this contest! What I really need is a mindless five-paragraph sort of entry: once upon a time, conflict, more conflict, climax, happily ever after.

I mean, if it's even possible. Possible *for me*.

Maybe I should ask Stella for advice? Because she cranks out these stories no problem!

Yeah, but if I did ask, I'm sure she'd act all stuck-up about it. Like: *Oh, poor Lyla, let me show you how it's done.* And anyway, I don't want to write like *her*; I want to write like *myself*! Myself when I'm feeling unstuck, I mean.

Okay, so what will get me unstuck?

I try that breathing thing Ms. Bowman told me about, inhaling for four seconds. Holding my breath for seven. Exhaling for eight. Then again. Then a third time.

Nothing.

So obviously it's not some sort of magical incantation.

I take a walk around the library for exercise. Ms. Rosen is talking to an eighth-grade teacher; if she notices me, she doesn't show it.

And now I give myself five minutes to gestate. Not a second longer than that, because THERE'S A DEADLINE, LYLA.

I rip out the smeary page, wrinkled and puckered with hand sweat.

All right, here we go, I tell myself. *Five minutes to clear your head, and then five simple paragraphs. Nothing to do with Aster and Verbena, Scribes and Vanguards, Defectors and sidekicks! Because there are tons of other stories, right? If you're a real writer, you should be able to think of hundreds, Lyla! Zillions!*

By the time the bell rings for lunch, I'm still Krazy-Glued to the chair, staring at the blindingly empty page.

"Lyla?"

Ms. Rosen is standing by my table. Today she's wearing a tee that says READ BANNED BOOOOOKS, and her earrings are shaped like ghosts.

Why ghosts? Oh, right. It's October 31. Halloween.

"Didn't you hear the bell?" she asks sweetly. "The period's over, and I think it's time for your lunch."

So she did notice me after all.

I shut my notebook so she won't see the blank page. "I know, but I need to stay here to work. Ms. Bowman said I could."

"Yes, but I'm sure she doesn't want you to skip lunch."

"Couldn't I just borrow another granola bar . . . ?"

"A granola bar is a snack, not a whole meal. If you finish your lunch before the end of the period, you can always return for a bit. Okay?"

Ms. Rosen is being nice, but also stubborn. If I argue with her, I'll just be wasting time. Which I'm running out of very fast.

I grab my notebook and race to the lunchroom.

EVIL SPELL

I get the quickest, easiest lunch they have—a container of vanilla yogurt and an apple—and head over to the usual spot with Journey.

I'm halfway across the lunchroom when I realize that she's sitting with Noah. Or rather, Noah is sitting with her.

Seeing the two of them together, chatting and smiling, makes me happy. But also . . . I can't help feeling a bit left out. Which is stupid, because it's not their fault I was hiding in the library.

As I take the empty seat next to Journey, she peeks at

me from under her cap. "Everything okay, Lyla? Noah said you weren't in ELA."

"I just went to work on my submission. You know, for the writing contest. Tomorrow's the deadline, so." I pull the foil off the top of my yogurt.

"Yeah, Orion already submitted his story," Noah says. "I only read the first part, but it's incredible."

"Well, I've read some of Lyla's, and it's *great* so far," Journey says.

My face burns. "Thanks, but it's not what I'm submitting."

"How come?" Noah asks.

I explain that all I have is a messy bunch of random scenes. "So I'm trying to write something short and contesty. But I can't think of anything, and it's driving me crazy."

Journey takes a bite of her grilled-cheese sandwich. "Why are you doing it, then?"

"I told you, Journey, it's very important to me!"

"I remember, but you never explained *why*. All you said was that your sister won second prize."

"She did?" Noah says. "When?"

I swallow a spoonful of yogurt. "Five years ago. For a poem about clouds."

Journey doesn't take her eyes off my face. "Lyla, you're a *writer*," she says. "You don't need to prove it to your sister. Or some contest judge. Or anyone else!"

I eat more yogurt.

"And I thought your writing was going better lately," she continues. "So why are you forcing yourself to write something different? I mean besides your story, which is what you really *want* to write. What you *need* to write. Isn't that what you keep telling me?"

I can't explain how this happens, but when Journey says these words, it's almost like she's reversing an evil spell. The lunchroom fades—all the tables and the meatloaf smells, all the clattering dishes and the laughing and talking. And now across my brain there's just one giant flashing message: *Journey is right. You really* don't *need to do this, Lyla. You aren't stuck.*

Because all the reasons I had for entering the contest, all the things I've been telling myself, over and over, these past few weeks, suddenly vaporize into nothing. Who cares what Rania's friends think, anyway? If they're mean to Journey, why should I bother trying to impress them? And if Rania's fine with their behavior, she won't change her opinion just because I've won some contest. She won't change her opinion of me, either, probably.

As for Dahlia: What's the point of competing with her? So I can win the trophy for Most Stressed-Out Student? And then toss it to go rescue sea turtles? Besides, the whole gap-year thing showed I can be tougher than my big sister, so what more would winning first prize prove, anyway?

Also, what I told Ms. Bowman about wanting readers: that's another garbage reason to enter the contest. I mean, I already have a great reader: Journey. I bet Noah, too, if I asked. Also Stella (if I really wanted).

Not to mention Ms. Bowman, who keeps offering. Ms. Bowman, who said her goal was for us to *enjoy* the writing process. Not torture ourselves for no reason.

It's almost like I forgot why I was writing in the first place: because I had a story in my head. A really, really good one. That I loved, and wanted to share with people.

I look up. Journey and Noah are watching me with serious eyes.

"Okay, forget the contest," I tell them. "Let's talk about something more interesting."

"Like what?" Noah asks.

I grin at my friends. "Nigel the hedgehog," I say.

WINNERS

I'm not going to lie: the day the writing contest winners are announced, I do feel a tiny stab of jealousy.

Okay, maybe not so tiny.

But when Ms. Bowman tells the class about Orion winning first prize for a story called "Day of the Droids," and Stella winning honorable mention for "A Feast with Grandma," I smile and cheer. Everyone else in the class claps politely, and some people don't clap at all; it's no secret that Stella isn't popular, but still, it bothers me that people aren't being nicer.

At the end of class I go over to congratulate her.

"Oh, thank you," she says. Her eyes dart away like she's embarrassed. "But it's just honorable mention."

It's weird how I'm sorry for her. I mean, honorable mention means the judges liked her story, but even so, I can tell she feels like a loser.

"Would it be okay if I read it?" I ask.

Stella blinks. "You don't have to, Lyla."

"But I really want to." The next thing I say surprises me. "Because I tried to write something for the contest, but I couldn't think of anything."

"Actually, I do have an extra copy," she admits, as she opens a folder the color of Pepto-Bismol. "Here. It's not my best. But I hope it helps you, Lyla."

"Thanks," I say. "I bet it will."

She smiles, and I smile back.

"It's called the *arribada*," Dahlia is telling Journey as we sit in the kitchen munching on potato chips. "Which means 'arrival.' And what I read is that between March and November, when the moon is full, the sea turtles crawl out from the ocean to lay eggs on the beaches. Thousands of turtles, each laying hundreds of eggs!"

"Whoa," Journey says. Her eyes are enormous as she

stares at the photo on Dahlia's laptop. "I didn't know sea turtles laid so many."

"Well, they have to, because there are so many natural predators, including vultures and dogs. Look at this." Dahlia clicks on some website. "Costa Rica has five species: the olive ridley, green sea turtle, loggerhead, hawksbill, and leatherback. . . ."

I'm really happy that Dahlia got into the six-month Costa Rica program. I'm happy she's so excited, and that she looks and sounds like Dahlia again. But this gap-year program thing is all she ever talks about these days—and if I have to listen to one more fact about sea turtles, I swear, I'm going to lose it.

But of course, Journey is fascinated about anything to do with animals, and I feel guilty about pulling her away. So after a few minutes I ask if it's okay if I go upstairs to read Stella's story.

"Sure," Journey says. "I just want to watch this one video anyway."

"Omigod, you *have* to!" Dahlia shouts as she opens another page. "Check this out, Journey: here's the beach in Ostional, where they had the largest ever arribada. . . ."

I pull Stella's story out of my backpack and take it upstairs to my room.

❀ ❀ ❀

Stella's story is about her grandma cooking a big feast for the family. I like reading about the recipes, how everyone argues about the ingredients, and how the grandma chases everyone out of the kitchen. But it just kind of ends—the family sits down at the table, the grandma tells them to eat before the food gets cold, and that's basically it.

So it's not exactly my kind of story. But I can tell it means a lot to Stella, because it's basically about how much she loves her family. And as I'm reading, I feel guilty for expecting it to be boring—for expecting anything about it, and about Stella, too.

Plus, I have to admit it's a big deal that Stella finished three stories when I couldn't finish a single one. And even though she still gets on my nerves sometimes, I can't stop thinking about her face when she won honorable mention. How kids in the class barely cheered when Ms. Bowman announced it.

"Okay, I finished," Journey says as she walks into my bedroom and plops on the bed next to Spumoni. "You're lucky, Lyla: your sister is so cool, and really smart. I bet you'll miss her when she's in Costa Rica!"

I know it sounds funny, but this is when it hits me for the first time: *Dahlia will be leaving soon.* What will that be

like for our family? No more fighting, no more drama, probably. And I'll have all of Mom and Dad's attention. Which will
be either good or bad. Or possibly somewhere in the middle.

"Yes, I'll definitely miss her, but I hope we get to visit,"
I reply. Then I pause. "Journey, can I ask you a big favor?"

CEREMONY

J ourney agrees to come with me to the awards ceremony,
even though she doesn't get the point.

"Won't you feel bad you didn't win?" she asks.

"Probably," I admit.

"Then why . . . ?"

To be honest, I can't explain why. It just feels right to
go—to cheer when they say Stella's name, to listen when
Orion reads his story. And yes, I definitely do expect to be
jealous, so it's a relief that Journey will go with me.

The ceremony is at the town library the following Saturday afternoon. As soon as we arrive in the lobby, I spot a giant poster propped up on an easel, with all the winners' names and the titles of their entries. I'm reading about the "personal memoirs" (aren't all memoirs personal?) when Ms. Bowman taps me on the shoulder.

"Lyla," she says, her eyes crinkling. "It's lovely to see you here."

I don't know why I feel embarrassed, but I do. "Yeah. I didn't submit something after all."

"That's okay. Maybe next year."

"Maybe. Anyway, I just thought I should come. For Stella."

If she remembers the stuff I said about Stella, she doesn't show it. "You're a good classmate, Lyla. And a good friend." She leans toward me. "So how's it going with your story?"

"Pretty good, actually. I decided to skip all that in-the-beginning stuff and just write the fun stuff in the middle. So now I've already filled a whole notebook. But lately . . ." I shrug. "I haven't written very much this week. I guess I've been taking a little break."

"Ah. Well, breaks are an essential part of the creative process. Right up there with cookies." She laughs. "Excuse me while I go raid the refreshment table."

Journey and I watch her walk off.

"She's really nice," Journey says.

"Better than nice," I reply. "She's my favorite teacher ever! You wanna hear something amazing? She plays bass in a rock band."

"Seriously?"

"Yeah. And she told me that when she gets stuck in her songwriting, she walks her dog. Or eats cookies."

"*Cookies?*" Journey grins. "I never knew that helped."

"Me neither," I admit, grinning back at her.

But now I see that Rania is heading in our direction. My smile freezes and my stomach bounces.

She's wearing her tie-dye Dickinson sweatshirt. And she looks pretty, just like always. Although is her hair a little shorter? I think maybe it is.

"*Oh,*" I say. Can she tell I'm rattled? "Hi, Rania."

"Hi, Lyla," she answers quietly. "I'm sorry you didn't win."

"Because she didn't *enter*," Journey says. Her voice has a sharp edge I've never heard before.

It's a weird moment I don't know what to do with. So I introduce them to each other, even though it's obviously not necessary. Then I explain to Rania that I'm here to cheer on Stella.

"Cool," Rania says. "I'm here for Orion. He showed me his story. It's really good."

"Yeah, Noah liked it too," I say.

"Who's Noah?"

"Our friend," Journey says. Although for some reason she says it like *frrriend*.

The three of us stand there. I shove my hands in my pockets.

Then Journey pokes my elbow. "Hey, Lyla, there's Noah over by the refreshment table. I'll go say hello. You want a doughnut or something?"

"No thanks." As I watch her walk off, I know she's not abandoning me, just giving me privacy with Rania. But still, with my mind a complete blank, I'm feeling something close to writing panic.

Rania's eyes meet mine. What is she expecting from me right now? I used to be able to read her thoughts. But not anymore, I guess.

"Okay, so," I say. "I think they'll be starting the ceremony soon. I guess we should take our seats?"

"Lyla, can I please say something first? I'm very sorry. I mean, for everything that happened between us."

"Forget it, okay?" Inside my pocket is an old gum

wrapper, which I roll into a tiny, hard ball. "We both just made other friends."

"Which is *supposed to* happen, right?"

"I guess. Anyway, it's what you told me once. Remember?"

Over Rania's shoulder I see Journey eating a doughnut while she's chatting with Noah. It's too far away to see what kind of doughnut, but the way she likes messy food, I'm guessing jelly. Or Boston cream.

Suddenly I have an urge to get a doughnut too. The funny thing is I don't even like doughnuts.

Rania is staring at my face. "You want to go to your friends," she says softly. "That's okay, Lyla, go ahead. I really just . . . wanted to say hello."

"Rania?"

"Yes?"

"You want to sit with us?"

"You mean with your friends?"

I nod. And seriously, it's not like I don't get the fact that I'm inviting Rania to be with *my* friends when I didn't want to be with *hers*.

Her eyebrows knit. She takes a second to answer.

"Okay, sure," she says, although she sounds the opposite of sure.

TROPHY

We all take seats in the fourth row: Noah, then Journey, then me, then Rania. It's definitely strange sitting so close to Rania. One time our knees bump by accident and we both apologize. In the old days we wouldn't have apologized—we'd have *expected* to bump into each other—so the apologies make me a little sad.

Two rows ahead, Stella sits with her family and Ms. Bowman. When Stella turns around to peek at the audience, I wave. She grins at me and waves back.

The head judge goes to the mic to welcome everyone.

He says that this year they had over a hundred entries, a record for the contest. Then he invites Orion to share his first-prize story, "Day of the Droids."

Orion gets up and walks to the mic. His voice is loud, but it trembles a little as he reads:

"'In the year 2500, no one can tell if you're human. So this means I'm able to slip in undetected. . . .'"

It's a really good story. I mean, *really* good. Better than Aster and Verbena—although it's probably not fair to compare them, because they're so different, really. Also, Orion's story is short, and mine . . . well, like I told Ms. Bowman, I've already filled a notebook. Which is an extremely big deal I should feel proud about, right? I mean, considering all the time I was stuck.

Still, listening to Orion read, I feel a definite pang— maybe not a *stab*, but it hurts anyway. I think Journey senses it too, because she gives my arm a small squeeze.

The ceremony takes about an hour. After Orion finishes, an eighth-grade girl reads the second-prize winner, a personal memoir about visiting her dad in hospice. Then a sixth grader reads the third-prize winner, a poem called "Trees" about . . . well, trees. After that the judges announce the honorable mentions, and everyone claps. Finally the winners get their money and their trophies as a photographer takes their pictures for the newspaper.

This is when Rania announces she's leaving to go meet Ayana and Gracie. I almost ask her to wait so she can congratulate Orion, but I don't want to start another whole argument about her friends.

So all I say is, "Okay, see you, Rania."

"See you, Lyla," she answers, flashing a smile. And then she speed-walks out of the library.

When the photos are done, I go to congratulate Stella. Then Noah, Journey, and I head over to Orion.

His face is glowing, but sweaty. "I was so nervous, I think I messed up reading," he says.

"No you didn't!" I shout. "You sounded *great*, Orion! And your story is *incredible!*"

Noah grins at me. "Exactly like I told you, right?"

"Even better than that!"

"Well, thank you, Lyla." Orion is looking past me. "Where's Rania? I thought I saw her here before."

"She had to leave," I say. "Family plans or something. But I know she loved your story too!"

This is when I realize that Ms. Bowman is standing a few steps away, watching us like she doesn't want to interrupt.

She catches my eye. "Can we please talk a sec, Lyla?" she asks.

I follow her to the easel. She hands me a piece of paper folded into a small, neat rectangle.

"Read it later," she murmurs. "Not here. All right?"

I nod and stick the rectangle in my pocket.

RECTANGLE

When I get home, Mom and Dad are in the kitchen, drinking tea and eating chocolate chip cookies. Real ones, just baked.

I breathe in chocolate-flavored air as I choose two big cookies off the baking sheet.

"Hey, sweetie," Mom says. "Dinner's in an hour, so don't fill up on those, please."

"I won't, I promise." I wrap the cookies in a napkin. "Thanks for baking."

"Thank your sister," Dad says. He grins. "She made

them with her friends. All *we* did was clean up afterward."

I stop myself from asking why Dahlia couldn't just clean up on her own. Again it hits me that in a few months, Dahlia won't be here to be babied and fussed over. What will it be like to have all the parent attention for myself? It's hard to know how to think about it; I guess I'll just have to find out.

Mom sips her tea. "So how was that library thing?"

"Great," I say.

And the funny thing is that it's not even a lie. It actually felt good to cheer for Stella and Orion. Even sitting with Rania wasn't so terrible. Probably nothing changed between us, and probably it never will—but it was good to know I could see her again and chat a little, and survive.

I walk past the living room, where Dahlia is on the sofa with Sophie and Nico.

"Hey, thanks for making cookies," I say loudly.

"Shh, Lyla, we're concentrating," Dahlia says. She doesn't take her eyes off the screen: *BeforeTimes VI* again. "Take a controller if you want to play."

"Yeah, join us," Sophie says.

"Maybe later," I answer, smiling.

I go up to my bedroom, plop on the bed next to Spumoni, and take the folded paper rectangle out of my pocket.

I read:

> *Dear Lyla,*
>
> *Remember, you don't write to win a trophy. You write because you love to, and because there's a story you want to tell. That's the prize you give yourself, and it's the only one that matters.*
>
> *Also, never forget all the people who are rooting for you—your friends, your family, and your teachers. We're here to help if you ever get stuck. When you get stuck, because getting stuck is part of the process. Along with breaks and cookies. ☺*
>
> *So keep your sidekicks close, okay? And if you never give up, if you keep writing (and reading!!), I know you'll make it through any quagmire.*
>
> *Love,*
>
> *Ms. Bowman*

I read the note three more times. Then I fold it back into a tiny rectangle and stick it in my desk drawer.

I eat both cookies. The chocolate chips are warm and melty. Yum.

I breathe: four, seven, eight.

And now I open my notebook to write my feelings.

TWENTY-FIVE WAYS TO GET UNSTUCK

Like every writer, I get stuck sometimes. Here are some strategies that have helped me work through writer's block. I hope they help you too!

1. Tell yourself that every writer deals with writer's block at some point (often at several points!). If you have writer's block, all it means is that you're a real writer. Welcome to the club!

2. Give yourself time to gestate; then jump in with both feet. Trust that ideas will come as you're working. You don't need to have it all figured out before you begin.

3. Read books in the same genre to give you ideas and techniques. Read books in other genres to help clear your head. Read, read, read! You can't write unless you read.

4. Because I write a lot of dialogue, whenever I'm stuck I like to read screenplays of my favorite movies and TV shows. Reading screenplays can help you "hear" how characters talk.

5. If you're having trouble getting started, consider writing from the middle. Or write scenes out of order.

6. Draw family trees and maps. Read baby-naming websites. This kind of procrastination can actually be helpful, as long as it doesn't go on for too long.

7. Share your work (even if it's not "ready") with teachers, classmates, friends, family. Embrace constructive feedback, especially if you're hearing the same reactions from several people.

8. Repeat to yourself: *First drafts don't need to be perfect—they just need to be written.* Most writing is rewriting. You'll have plenty of chances later to make it better.

9. Try to resist self-editing as you write. Giving yourself ten minutes of free writing at the start of a writing session may help to warm up your writing muscles.

10. Relocate. A change of scenery often helps.

11. Do mindful breathing to de-stress: four, seven, eight.

12. Exercise. If you have a dog, take her outside for a long walk. If you're writing at school, get up from your desk and move around the room.

13. Play word games. Do word-search puzzles, crosswords, Spelling Bees, Wordle, etc.

14. Resist the urge to compare yourself to published authors. Try to avoid comparing yourself to anyone, including classmates.

15. If you imagine someone looking over your shoulder as you write, or if you hear critical voices, try to banish them. They aren't there to help.

16. For some writers, deadlines help them focus. If you're the sort of writer who hates deadlines, forget about the calendar, and work where you won't notice the clock.

17. Write your feelings.

18. Consider switching perspectives, especially from third person to first. If you're already writing in the first person, switch to another character's point of view.

19. Switch pens. Or switch to pencil. If you're writing by hand, type. If you're typing, write by hand. If you're writing in a notebook, switch to a legal pad. Changing habits and breaking negative associations can help.

20. Step away from your story. Write something else, or don't write anything. Listen to music. Watch a movie.

21. Describe the plot of your story to someone. Explain how and why you feel stuck. Talking always, always helps.

22. Leave blanks. You can always fill them in later.

23. Change the genre of your writing. If you're working on a story, try writing a scene in verse, or as a play.

24. Don't focus on contests, prizes, awards, or trophies. Don't think about impressing anyone. Don't even think about getting published. Try to enjoy the *process* of writing—that's the only prize that matters.

25. Eat cookies.

ACKNOWLEDGMENTS

Every book is a team effort, and once again I'm beyond lucky to work with the amazing folks of Aladdin: my wonderful editor, Alyson Heller, along with Kristin Gilson, Michelle Leo, Amy Beaudoin, Nicole Benevento, and Nia Todd. Karen Sherman, thanks for another terrific job of copyediting. Heather Palisi, thanks for the beautiful design. Erika Pajarillo, thanks for another gorgeous cover. I love making books with you all.

Jill Grinberg, I'm so grateful on a daily basis that you're my agent and my friend. Big thanks to everyone at Jill Grinberg Literary Management, especially Sam Farkas and Denise Page.

I'm also deeply grateful to Tracy van Straaten, Melissa Bloomfield, and Hannah Boardman of TvS Media Group for helping to launch this book into the world.

As Ms. Bowman says, every writer needs beta readers, and I was lucky to have two great ones: Eliza Hawthorne and Sunflower.

Most of all, thanks to my family: Chris, Josh, Alex and Dani, Lizzy and Jamie. Bonus thanks to Chris and Lizzy, who patiently read early drafts and, as always, made many hugely helpful suggestions. I love you all.

ABOUT THE AUTHOR

BARBARA DEE is the author of fourteen middle-grade novels published by Simon & Schuster, including *Haven Jacobs Saves the Planet*, *Violets Are Blue*, *My Life in the Fish Tank*, *Maybe He Just Likes You*, *Everything I Know About You*, *Halfway Normal*, and *Star-Crossed*. Her books have earned several starred reviews and have been named to many best-of lists, including the Washington Post Best Children's Books, the ALA Notable Children's Books, the ALA Rise: A Feminist Book Project List, the NCSS-CBC Notable Social Studies Trade Books for Young People, and the ALA Rainbow Book List Top Ten. Barbara is one of the founders of the Chappaqua Children's Book Festival. She lives with her family, including a naughty cat named Luna and a sweet rescue hound dog named Ripley, in Westchester County, New York.